...aristocrat Cedric Pemberton, it's time for the
Pemberton heirs to stake their claim in the family
empire.

From fashion and cosmetics to jewelry and
fragrance, Aurora Inc. is a multinational company,
with headquarters all over the world.

As the siblings take the lead in different divisions
of the business, they'll face challenges, uncover
secrets and learn to start listening to their hearts...

We hope you enjoy Will and Gabi's story,
and return for more Pemberton adventures in
Aurora Inc., coming soon!

Dear Reader,

When the new year rolls around, do you have a word of the year? I know a lot of people do, and while I don't personally come up with one word as a "guide," lately I've been thinking a lot about life and what I want it to look like. What I've come up with is *joy*.

We all have to do things we don't want to do, but now, when I think about decisions I must make, I consider if the outcome will bring me joy or not. It's been wonderful having joy as the goal! It's clarified so much of my thinking!

Joy is something I've been looking to reconnect with, so it's even more lovely that I've found writing this new series, Heirs to an Empire, quite joyful. Brainstorming it with my friends was so fun it was ridiculous. There's drama, family secrets, gorgeous settings and, of course, falling in love.

Everyone has their share of troubles and strife, but at the end of the day, if there are moments of joy, it makes it all worth it. I hope you en*joy* this story, and come back for more Pemberton and Aurora, Inc. adventures.

Happy reading,

Donna

Scandal and the Runaway Bride

Donna Alward

HARLEQUIN

Romance

ISBN-13: 978-1-335-55647-9

Scandal and the Runaway Bride

Copyright © 2020 by Donna Alward

All rights reserved. No part of this book may be used or reproduced in
any manner whatsoever without written permission except in the case of
brief quotations embodied in critical articles and reviews.

This is a work of fiction. Names, characters, places and incidents
are either the product of the author's imagination or are used fictitiously.
Any resemblance to actual persons, living or dead, businesses,
companies, events or locales is entirely coincidental.

This edition published by arrangement with Harlequin Books S.A.

For questions and comments about the quality of this book,
please contact us at CustomerService@Harlequin.com.

Harlequin Enterprises ULC
22 Adelaide St. West, 40th Floor
Toronto, Ontario M5H 4E3, Canada
www.Harlequin.com

Printed in U.S.A.

Donna Alward lives on Canada's east coast with her family, which includes her husband, a couple of kids, a senior dog and two crazy cats. Her heartwarming stories of love, hope and homecoming have been translated into several languages, hit bestseller lists and won awards, but her favorite thing is hearing from readers! When she's not writing, she enjoys reading (of course), knitting, gardening, cooking... and she is a *Masterpiece Theatre* addict. You can visit her on the web at donnaalward.com and join her mailing list at donnaalward.com/newsletter.

Books by Donna Alward

Harlequin Romance

South Shore Billionaires

Christmas Baby for the Billionaire
Beauty and the Brooding Billionaire
The Billionaire's Island Bride

Destination Brides

Summer Escape with the Tycoon

Marrying a Millionaire

Best Man for the Wedding Planner
Secret Millionaire for the Surrogate

Heart to Heart

Hired: The Italian's Bride

How a Cowboy Stole Her Heart

Visit the Author Profile page
at Harlequin.com for more titles.

To the real sister wives, Barb, Shirley, Jenna and Renee—brainstormers extraordinaire and the best besties in the world.

Praise for
Donna Alward

"A stellar contemporary romance that is simply outstanding, *Christmas Baby for the Billionaire* is a wonderful story I loved losing myself in. Donna Alward is a terrific storyteller who is always on top form and in her latest romance, she has penned a story of hope, second chances, healing and new beginnings peppered with humor and pathos that is absolutely impossible to put down."

—*Goodreads*

CHAPTER ONE

Surrey, mid-July

WILLIAM PEMBERTON HELD the folded sheet of cream paper in his hand and clenched his jaw. Just beyond this room, in the Chatsworth estate chapel, his elder brother, Stephen Pemberton, the Earl of Chatsworth, was waiting for his bride. The guests had already filled the pews and the organist was playing quietly, though the wait had been so long now she was starting to repeat pieces. The bridesmaids were lined up at the entry doors, dresses and bouquets perfect, and William had been discreetly dispatched to find out what was keeping the bride.

What he'd discovered was no bride at all, and a note instead.

I'm sorry. Please forgive me.

William fought to contain the rage and contempt racing through his veins. His brother was a good man, and deserved better than this. Especially after his previous broken engagement—though the rest of the family wasn't aware of the circumstances of Stephen's breakup with Bridget. Only William, who'd found his brother soundly inebriated in the Chatsworth study one night last February, knew the truth. The whole sordid tale had come out over far too much gin.

And while William had thought that Stephen's marriage to Gabriella was also a mistake, this was too much. Who did Gabi Baresi think she was? There'd been ample time to change her mind. Instead she'd left it to the eleventh hour, when it was sure to humiliate Stephen—and his family—the most. Rage simmered in William's veins. This wasn't just going to hurt Stephen, it was going to be a PR nightmare for Aurora, Inc.

He let out a breath. Okay. His job right now was damage control. There would be no wedding today and he had to think fast to keep it from being an utter scandal, splashed all over the tabloids. The Pembertons and the company didn't need that. Not now, so soon after William's father's death.

He folded the paper in little squares, tucked it into his pocket, and then set his shoulders, preparing for the horrible task ahead. His shoes clicked on the stone floor as he made his way through the back door to the chapel, where Stephen looked over at him with a questioning brow.

William gave a jerk of his head and Stephen hurried to his side, still beaming his happy groom smile. That was, until they were behind a gigantic display of roses and lilies. William nearly choked on the overpowering scent.

"What is it?" Stephen asked. "You look like you're ready to murder someone."

"Not far off," William whispered. "Listen, Gabi's not coming. But I have a plan, so please don't go off half-cocked until you hear me out."

Stephen's face paled and his lips thinned. "My God. What do you mean, she's not coming?"

"She left a note, saying she's sorry and to forgive her."

"Let me see it."

William had learned long ago to never disobey that tone in his brother's voice. He took the note out of his pocket and unfolded it, careful to keep it out of sight of any guests. Not much worry, though. There were so many flower arrangements that the chapel had become a veritable bower of blooms. One only had to duck behind a single installment of blossoms and greenery to be completely concealed.

Stephen swore.

"My thoughts exactly," William said. "Now, here's what you're going to do, and it's going to take all your acting ability. You're going to go up to that altar, incredibly concerned that your bride-to-be has fallen horribly ill. You're going to ask to be excused, and you're going to go back to the house. No one is going to see you, and once I've found her we'll figure out a plan to contain the damage. It'll be on social media within the hour, so we have to watch our steps."

"You're going to find her."

"Oh, yes," William promised darkly. "I don't care if we have to call it food poisoning or the flu, but she is going to disappear for a while to 'recuperate' until this is under control. Then you can decide if you still want to go through with this farce."

"William—"

"I know. Sorry. We'll talk more later. Right now, you give the performance of your life and get back to the house. I'll smooth things here and then find Gabi."

Stephen gave a brusque nod. If William had ever had any doubts about his brother's feelings for Gabi, they were put to rest. He was angry, but he wasn't heartbroken like a man should be when his bride pulls a runner. It was small comfort, but it was something.

Stephen went to the altar and cleared his throat. "Ladies and gentlemen, I'm so sorry to say that there won't be a wedding today. Gabi has fallen horribly ill. I thank you all for coming, and I'm sure we'll set a new date once she's feeling better. Right now, I'd better go look after my…after Gabriella." He put on an expression of appropriate concern and affection that even William nearly believed.

Then Stephen brushed past him and stormed through the door, looking to the rest of the world like a worried fiancé. But William knew that look. And when Stephen wore that expression, his mind was set. No matter what Gabi said now, this "arrangement" was over. Maybe that was a blessing, even if it was a mess to be cleaned up.

Their mother, Aurora Germain Pemberton, hastened forward, concern flattening her normally soft, ethereal expression. "William, what is happening?"

He met her gaze and kept his voice low. "Gabi ran. Stephen's going to the house as if she's ill. I'm going to find her, and then I'm going to find us a way out of this mess. Can you handle things here? Say as little as possible?"

She scoffed. "Of course." Then she looked up at William. "I wish I could say I was sorry, but I'm not. She was not the woman for Stephen, and they do not love each other. But, *mon Dieu*, I wish she'd done it another way. What a mess."

"I know, *Maman*." He risked a little of Stephen's secret. "You know he wanted a happy occasion. Something to make you look to the future, instead of grieving so much."

Aurora looked into William's eyes, and he saw the sadness lurking in the gray depths. "Grief is what it is, darling. I will always grieve for your father. No wedding can take that away."

"I'm sorry."

"Don't be. It is life." She smiled a little and kissed his cheek. "Now, don't worry about a thing here. This is not my first PR crisis."

She walked away, head high and so very poised. His mother was an incredibly strong woman.

One of the bridesmaids was standing back, twisting her fingers in her bouquet and biting her lip. Gabi's younger sister, Giulia, who had traveled from Italy to be in the wedding. William beckoned her forward.

"Giulia, right?" he asked.

She nodded, chewing on her lip even more. She was young, maybe twenty-two or so. And Gabi had abandoned her, too. William might have felt sorry for her except he didn't have the luxury of sympathy at the moment. A young man hovered just behind her—well, maybe Giulia wasn't totally alone. She'd brought a plus one with her, though Will couldn't remember his name.

"Is my sister all right?"

"Did you speak to her this morning?"

Giulia nodded quickly. "Yes, of course. She was nervous, but who isn't on their wedding day?"

William searched her face for any hint of lying and found nothing. He was generally good at reading people, and he wasn't sure this sweet young woman had it in her to be manipulative or a liar.

"Come with me," he said, putting his hand on her arm. "Where we can speak more privately."

The young man stepped forward, but Giulia gave a quick shake of her head and he halted. Her heels clacked behind William's black dress shoes as he led her out of the chapel and into the room where he'd found the note. He shut the door behind him and looked her square in the eye. "Your sister isn't sick. She left a note and ran."

"Oh, *Dio mio!*"

William lifted an eyebrow. "That's a common sentiment at the moment." So far he'd heard it in three languages.

"Do you know where she is? Oh, no." Giulia's hand was now over her mouth, her bouquet dangling from her opposite hand. "I need to go to her…"

While William believed Giulia's upset was genuine, he wasn't swayed by her distressed voice. "Actually, I was hoping you might know where I could find her. This is quite a mess. We don't want news to get out, do we? Did she say anything to you? Anything at all?"

"I don't understand." Giulia gave a sniff, and William patiently went to the desk and retrieved a tissue for her.

She dabbed her nose and eyes, and then William started again. "Giulia, your sister and my brother were getting married for appearances only. We both know they are not in love. Marrying Stephen meant that your family's struggling company would benefit from an alliance with Aurora. Surely you must see how that won't happen now."

Her eyes widened and he felt like the world's biggest heel. He hadn't said anything that was a lie, but he was being cold and calculating right now. It wasn't his usual way of doing things. This was what came of having had to do far too much crisis management since his father died.

"But… Mama and Papa…this isn't their fault."

He gentled his voice. "No, of course not. But until I find Gabi and we sort this out…" He let the thought hang, and watched as Giulia sorted through the ramifications on her own.

"William…" She said his name hesitantly, as if unsure if she was being too familiar. "Please, I… I do want to help. She is my sister."

"There are two ways you can help," he said firmly. "The first is to not breathe a word about this to anyone. If it gets out that she left Stephen at the altar, I promise you there will not be a deal with your family. Ever."

She nodded quickly.

"The second is to help me find her. Do you know where she might have gone? Is there anyone she would go to or a place that comes to mind?"

She shook her head rapidly, then paused. "London. She'd try to hide in London. She always said that a person could get lost there. We laughed about it. Our city is much smaller."

"That's not a lot to go on."

Giulia met his gaze. "I don't know. She joked all the time about staying at the Ritz like Julia Roberts in that movie, you know? Where she always used a cartoon character as a fake name?"

William fought the urge to roll his eyes. Yes, *Notting Hill*. His sister Arabella had watched it often enough.

The Ritz wasn't a lot to go on, but it was a place to start.

He ripped a corner off the note and grabbed a pen from the vicar's desk. "If you hear from her or think of anything, please let me know." He jotted down his mobile number. "I can't help her if I can't find her."

And he did want to help her. Only because that was the singular way to help his family.

And he'd do anything for them.

Gabriella's hands trembled as she lifted the demitasse to her lips. If they were at Chatsworth Hall, Stephen would have called for restorative tea. But tea wasn't for Gabi, not at this moment. What she required was several jolts of espresso so she could make a better plan.

· She'd left him. Fled Surrey in her wedding dress and in Stephen's car. She'd left the car at the train station, taken her bag and changed into regular clothes before hopping on the train for London. She had never done anything this impulsive in her life—and that included agreeing to marry Stephen in the first place.

Her couture dress was stuffed into a garment bag and was hanging in the closet where she couldn't see it. So far the only thing she'd been capable of was getting to the room and ordering coffee. Her hands wouldn't stop shaking and her stomach quaked as she thought about what she'd done and the consequences.

What would happen to Baresi Textiles? Her parents? Her baby sister, whom she'd left behind at the estate? Though at least Giulia had Marco. She wasn't alone.

Gabi put the small cup down on the table and rested her forehead on her hands. She'd ruined everything. But how could she have gone through with it? Marriage to a man she didn't love? An agreement to bear a child…to divorce…all for financial gain?

It had been a dumb idea. She should have had the courage to say no from the beginning. She'd been so very worried about her father and hiding her own broken heart, but that was no excuse for making stupid decisions. At least she could try to make things right now.

When she thought of Stephen, her gut twisted again. He wasn't a bad man. He was nice, and incredibly handsome, and he'd always treated her with respect and kindness. He'd been easy to like. But not love. The chemistry wasn't there. And maybe that had been the clincher. He had been very open about wanting a child to inherit the title that he'd inherited himself only a year ago. In the end, she hadn't been able to bring herself to sleep with someone she didn't at least desire.

Was it selfish? Maybe. It didn't really matter now. It was done. She'd ruined the wedding and Stephen's plan and his guarantees for her family's business.

And worst of all, she really didn't like herself at this moment. It had been a coward's move, and a panicked one. For a woman who considered herself strong and reasonable, jilting a groom at the altar was incredibly out of character.

Maybe, just maybe, that was indicative of her level of desperation, and not a horrible character flaw?

She'd just lifted the cup to her lips again when there was a knock at the door. Gabi frowned; she hadn't ordered anything else from room service and she hadn't told anyone where she was going. Not even Giulia.

A peek through the peephole showed William Pemberton, and her stomach turned to ice.

"Gabriella, I know you're inside. Open the door."

She swallowed against the lump in her throat.

"This is a hell of a mess you made. I'm here to help you."

"I doubt that." She finally opened her mouth and the words came out stronger than she'd anticipated. Good.

"Minimizing the damage from this helps you *and* Stephen. Now let me in."

"Is he with you?"

"No. Now open the door."

She did, because the last thing they needed was to be having a conversation with a door between them, where anyone passing in the hallway could hear.

He stepped inside and she shut the door behind him.

"Nice room."

She met his gaze. Oh, he was angry. So very angry, and he had a right to be. But she would stand her ground, too. Maybe it was messy but she'd done the right thing.

"I took a basic room, and not a suite, William."

"Still put it on my brother's card, though, didn't you?"

"Is that how you found me?" She didn't deny the card. Stephen had given it to her several weeks ago, to pay for things for the wedding. She'd planned to use it to get back to Italy and then pay him back every penny. She'd kept all the receipts.

"No," he answered. "I spoke to your sister."

Her gaze snapped to his and held. "I didn't tell her where I was going."

"She's your sister. She remembers things. Apparently there's a movie you like quite a bit, Cinderella."

The way he said it wasn't a compliment. And she supposed she deserved it. She'd run from her wedding like Cinderella had run from the ball. Only the prince wasn't the one roaming the countryside to find her. It was the younger brother of an earl.

"I couldn't do it, William. I couldn't marry him. Not when I don't…when we don't…" Her voice caught and she turned away, suddenly exhausted despite the injection of espresso.

He let out a sigh behind her. "Dammit, Gabi, I'm angry as hell. I like you, you know. I think you're a good person. I thought you two were making a mistake, but really? The day of the wedding, after everyone got to the chapel? Why wait so long?"

Tears pricked at her eyes. "I thought I could do it. Mama and Papa…they needed me to go through with the wedding. Having Aurora step in meant security for the business while my father is fighting…" She couldn't finish the sentence. Even saying the word *cancer* sent a sick feeling through her body. "Now I've ruined it all."

Afraid of losing her grip on her emotions, she went to the window and looked out over the city.

Daylight was softening, and she took a moment to breathe deeply and regain control. Then she turned around. "What happened at the chapel?"

"Stephen told everyone you'd fallen ill. It's to buy us some time before we need to make an announcement about rescheduling."

Alarm skittered down her spine. "Rescheduling? No, William, no… I can't do that. No, the wedding is off. I promise I'll pay back what I spent and…and…" And she thought about her ailing father going through cancer treatments, and how they'd stayed in Italy because he was too sick to make the trip for the wedding, and she finally broke down in the way she hadn't let herself in the weeks leading to this day. What if they lost the company? What if…he died?

Large hands settled on her shoulders and guided her to the table where the coffee service was set up. She sat in the chair and tried to regain her composure. Will sat opposite her and poured himself a cup of the espresso. "Take your time," he suggested. "I'm guessing you need to get that out."

She looked up at him through eyes blurred with tears. "Oh, so now you're nice?"

His dark gaze was steady. "Make no mistake, Gabi. I'm furious. But if you were upset enough to run from the wedding, I'm guessing there are some hefty emotions that need to get out. I'd prefer you do it now so we can make a plan without that messiness getting in the way."

So not so nice. Instead he was a cold, arrogant jerk. Hah. And she'd always thought him the fun one, and Stephen the serious one. No such luck.

He took out his phone and tapped in a message while she wiped her eyes on a thick white napkin. "What are you doing?"

"Telling Stephen to keep up the story that you're ill. And then I'm messaging your sister to tell her you're safe. You left her behind, too, you know. In a strange country where she doesn't know anyone."

She wasn't sure it was possible for a human to feel guiltier than she felt at this moment. "She has Marco with her, and a return ticket for Monday," she reminded him.

"Yes, and they are now staying at our house. How do you think she feels?"

Gabi got up from the table and spun away, irritation flaring. "Fine, William, I'm a horrible, horrible human. Is that what you want to hear?"

But neither tears nor temper fazed him. "All I'm saying is that there are a lot of moving parts to consider. As far as the world knows, you got food poisoning and were too sick to attend the wedding. We'll feed snippets to the press. And no one here will talk. I took care of that."

She resented him even more now. The Pembertons had the money and status to pull all that off, didn't they?

"Well, I guess you have it all under control." Even if she'd wanted to, she couldn't keep the sarcasm out of her voice.

"Not quite. Making this work means keeping you off the radar and away from the paparazzi. And that means you packing your bag again. You can't stay here."

She laced her fingers together, trying to control the unease trickling through her at his tone. "And where do you suggest I go?"

"Not you. *We*. I'm not letting you out of my sight. So why don't you order us some dinner while I sort out the arrangements?"

He turned away, effectively dismissing her. If she'd felt that her life was out of her control, she felt it even more intensely now. She was at the mercy of William Pemberton and his family. But she wouldn't be forever. She'd make sure of it.

CHAPTER TWO

IT WAS DARK when Gabi showed her passport and then followed William to the Aurora, Inc., private jet. Of course they wouldn't risk flying commercial and being seen. She was being escorted away like a dirty secret, hidden away until there was a plan to "deal" with the situation. The situation being her, of course.

She wanted to be angry about it. And maybe she should. But the truth was, this was a PR nightmare. And she was the one who'd caused it.

The inside of the jet was familiar, yet tonight she felt like an interloper. She'd flown in it before, of course. As Stephen Pemberton's fiancée, she'd flown from her home in Italy to Paris, and Stephen's luxurious flat there, and of course to London, where it was a short commute to Chatsworth Hall. Indeed, the plane had been fueled and ready for the honeymoon trip, a week on Malta.

She paused and William came up behind her, letting out a breath of frustration. "What is it now?"

"Sorry. I'll take my seat. Where are we going again?"

"To the château."

Right. He'd said France. She should have remembered, but she was exhausted and distracted by everything. As she sank into the buttery leather, she bit her lip. "For how long?"

He shrugged. "A few days, a week? Hard to say."

A week. She frowned. As long as she could be back home for her father's surgery, it would be okay.

William had been calling Stephen and the pilot and whoever else he'd needed to call. Gabi had only made two calls. One to her sister, and then one to her parents.

On the first call she'd been completely honest and apologized to Giulia for leaving her stranded. Giulia said the Pembertons were looking after her and not to worry. Of course that was what Giulia would say. She was the peacemaker of the family and would do anything to avoid conflict.

Her parents had been another story. She'd lied to them, and it had hurt. She'd perpetuated the story of her illness and setting a new date. The illness angle kept the call mercifully brief. The guilt, however, had settled like a lead weight in her stomach, and she wasn't sure it could ever be dislodged. She'd done so much more than lie to them today. She'd thrown away the chance to save their company. If she couldn't manage in her father's absence, they might have to sell, which would break his heart. Going into an early retirement was not his plan at all. The partnership with Aurora would have kept it financially stable while he went through his treatments and recovered. She was twenty-eight years old and held an accounting degree—how was she supposed to manage the entire company and navigate it through a tough economy?

Her throat closed over with emotion. She was going to disappoint people, and that hurt her heart.

"What are you thinking?" William asked, sitting across from her and reaching for his seat belt.

"I'm thinking that I've ruined everything. My parents…my arrangement with Stephen would have kept everything going and kept the company in my father's name. Now we're probably going to have to sell." She met William's gaze. "I feel like the most selfish woman on the planet. Even though deep down I know marrying Stephen would have been wrong."

"Would it have been so bad? Being a countess?"

"Maybe you don't believe me, but I don't care about those things. What is being a countess when one is miserable? Not that your brother is awful," she hurried to add. "But I'm not in love with him, and I can't imagine being married to someone I don't love. Even temporarily. I thought I could, but…" She turned away. "Oh, maybe I'm just naive. I probably sound silly and stupid."

"No, not that," William said. "I'm mad at you about the mess. But personally, I agree with you. The engagement was foolish. I can't actually believe that Stephen came up with the idea. He doesn't usually buckle to pressure. Not even from our mother."

The plane began to taxi down the runway and Gabi fastened her seat belt across her hips. "He loves her, and he loved his father. She's grieving for Cedric so much. He wanted to give her hope. A wedding and…and a baby. A grandchild to carry on her husband's legacy. Is that so bad?" Stephen had made a compelling case. Plus she'd always liked him. They'd first met three years ago. She'd been working with the Baresi accountant with the goal of taking over the financial aspect of the business eventually, and Stephen had been looking in on Aurora suppliers as he took on more responsibility within the company. Stephen had been charming and kind and they'd become friends. On his last trip, she'd confessed her worries to him over a glass or two…or maybe three…of Chianti. He'd come up with the plan.

And he'd said he trusted her because they were friends.

Her cheeks heated, though. Perhaps that was

the clincher in the whole decision, really. A marriage of convenience she might have been able to go through with. But bearing Stephen's child... She wanted children, of course she did. Very much. And Stephen was an honorable man who would honor his promises. But...

But. It always came down to the lack of actual love between them. It was completely platonic on her end, and she suspected on his, too. It was the one thing she couldn't talk herself around.

"It's not bad, as an idea. As a plan, though, it's very... I don't know. Like something out of those period dramas that Charlotte loves to watch."

His twin sister, Charlotte, was a doll. "I like your family very much," she said softly. "They've been very good to me. They must hate me right now."

"As far as they know, you've broken Stephen's heart and caused a scandal."

"Are you always so blunt?"

"Yes." But he smiled a little, and a light flickered in his eyes. "There isn't much room for misinterpretation when one speaks clearly and honestly."

"I'm not sure if I like it or not. But I thank you for not yelling at me. Or being...too angry."

They reached altitude and William unbuckled his seat belt and rose, moving to the onboard bar. He took out two glasses and poured a good splash of cognac in each. As he handed her the wide-bowled glass, he smiled. "I think you both dodged a bullet today. This, darling, is simply controlling the story. A week or so in Provence will keep you hidden away from the paparazzi. After that, you can set a new date." She was about to protest when he held up his free hand. "A date which will never happen. After an appropriate amount of time, the wedding will be quietly called off, you'll go your separate ways and that will be that."

So neat and tidy. Should she be grateful that William was taking care of all of it, or angry at having her life dictated yet again? "And what about Baresi Textiles?" she asked, lifting her chin.

He took a healthy sip of his cognac and lifted an eyebrow. "You'll have to ask Stephen his plans. And maybe wait until his pride's not in the toilet."

She sipped her drink, and it made her feel warm and slightly drowsy. She and William didn't talk anymore. He had taken out his phone and kept rapidly typing in messages. She was unbearably curious, and kept sliding glances his way.

He looked a little like his brother, but there was a difference, too, in the square set of his jaw. His hair was dark brown and cut short and neat, and if he would smile more his eyes would soften from a hard, cold golden brown to something that made her think of waving grasses in autumn fields, a little green, a little brown, but never quite one or the other. Right now he was still in his tuxedo trousers and shirt, though he'd undone the cuffs and rolled up the sleeves, and ditched the tie. The unbuttoned collar drew her eyes to a V of skin, right at the hollow of his throat.

She guessed him to be somewhere around six feet, and like the rest of his family, he had a lean legginess that led to a trim waist and a broader chest and shoulders.

All in all, the Pembertons were a good-looking family, and William was no exception.

It would have been so much easier if she could have actually loved Stephen. But then, he didn't want to be loved, so it didn't really matter.

She drank the last drop of cognac and leaned back against the soft seat. It wasn't long at all and her eyelids were drooping…

William frowned as he looked over at Gabi as she fell asleep. There was no big shifting to a comfortable position or snuffling or anything. She sat back, her lids grew heavy and she was gone.

Stephen was a fool. Gabriella Baresi was a beautiful woman: smart, a little shy, but what she'd done today? It was an almighty headache, but damn, it was brave. She would have made Stephen a great wife, if he'd let her. But Stephen was an idiot right now, still stinging from his last relationship gone wrong. While most would consider her last question to be cold and calculating, he didn't think so. She had been going through with this out of a sense of family loyalty and responsibility. Her father was ill. Aurora would have partnered with Baresi for the finest Italian cashmere, in exchange for her father still maintaining control of the company. Stephen had agreed, with his own preposterous conditions.

William shook his head. The pair of them, trying to live up to parental expectations in the most misguided way. Not that he didn't understand. He owed everything to both Stephen and their father. His life had been on a dangerous path until the two of them had stepped in and saved him. He hadn't deserved it. He'd acted like the typical "spare" to the heir, partying too much, getting attention the wrong way, getting in over his head. Stephen could have washed his hands of Will and his antics, but instead he'd stepped in and been Will's biggest support.

Saint Stephen. The old nickname flitted through his brain, and he frowned. Stephen always did everything right. Will constantly had to prove himself. But he'd brought that on himself, so he shuttered the feelings away and studied the sleeping woman across from him again.

He'd met Massimo Baresi. William seriously doubted that the man knew what bargain Gabi had struck to save their business. He was a proud, smart man going through a horrible time. No, Gabi had taken this on herself, and he thought back to his crack about being a countess. He didn't think she'd done it for her own personal gain. She'd accepted Stephen for the good of her family, a self-sacrifice. Misguided, but admirable.

He swallowed tightly. She *was* beautiful. There was no harm in admitting that; it was a fact and he was a fan of facts in general. A piece of hair curled around her heart-shaped face, the same sable color as her thick eyelashes. Her lashes were full and curled up slightly at the ends. Her mouth was relaxed in sleep, delicate lips a soft pink now that she'd chewed her lipstick off.

He'd learned she chewed on her lips when upset or nervous. She'd done it a lot today. Choosing to run hadn't been easy for her. He rather suspected she'd been pumped full of adrenaline all day. No wonder she'd crashed.

In an hour or so they'd be in France, headed to the Germain château, surrounded by lush gardens and lavender fields. It was the most beautiful place he'd ever been, and now he was going to be there with her for the next week.

At this point he didn't know if that was a curse or a blessing.

Coffee. The rich, thick, beautiful scent of it woke Gabi from a deep sleep. She blinked and then rolled over and gasped at the sight of a maid depositing a tray on a small table.

"*Oh, excusez-moi, mademoiselle.*" She stood and wiped her hands on her apron.

"You brought coffee. No need to beg pardon. You have my undying gratitude." She sat up a bit and pushed her hair back. "What's your name?"

"Suzanne," came the reply.

"*Merci*, Suzanne. I can't face the day without coffee."

They shared a smile and then the maid slipped away, closing the bedroom door with a click.

Good heavens. She didn't realize there'd be a maid. But then, the château was huge. Of course there was staff.

She barely remembered arriving last night. William had awakened her on landing and they'd been ushered into a car and then into the château sometime around two a.m.—or was it three? She reached for the coffee and inhaled its strong aroma, took a bracing sip and sighed as she leaned against the enormous headboard. Someone had guided her to this room and deposited her bags as well. The bags, still packed, now stood by a gorgeous wardrobe. She'd unpack this morning after…

She didn't know what after. She was supposed to be sick, wasn't she? And she highly doubted William wanted anything to do with her.

He'd have to, though. Because she insisted on

knowing about the mysterious "plan." Maybe she didn't have much control over what happened next, and for good reason, she admitted to herself. But she wasn't about to sit back and be quiet as a mouse about it, either.

She emptied her cup and filled it again, then sampled the flaky, rich croissant on the plate and picked at the fresh berries in a china bowl. Last night she'd barely touched her dinner, and now she found herself quite hungry. It wasn't long before the food had disappeared, the coffee had kicked in and she was ready for a shower and a fresh start.

It was amazing to think that yesterday at this time she'd been preparing to put on her wedding dress. It seemed as if it were days ago, and not a mere twenty-four hours.

She'd showered and dressed and was putting cream on her face when she realized she hadn't seen her mobile this morning.

She dashed back to the bedroom and ripped through her handbag. No phone. She lugged her suitcase to the bed, threw it on top of the coverlet and opened it, tossing clothing aside looking for the tiny piece of tech that kept her connected to her life. Nothing. She hung the garment bag that held the wedding dress, now crumpled, in the wardrobe and tried to calm her heartbeat. Had she left it on the plane, perhaps? In the car last night? She tried to remember where she had it last and couldn't think.

"Good heavens."

Her head snapped up at the sound of William's voice. He stood in the doorway, staring at the state of her room, his mouth agape. She followed his gaze.

Her clothes were strewn all over the room. Dresses and skirts littered the fine silk of the coverlet, shoes and trousers were scattered all over the floor, and her cheeks heated as she realized a few of her very fine and pretty underthings were tossed over a tufted chair.

She lifted her chin. "I'm unpacking."

William lifted one eyebrow and she would swear his eyes twinkled with amusement, despite his stern expression. "An unorthodox method."

She wouldn't laugh. She was too vulnerable right now to attempt to share any sort of camaraderie with him. "I'm sorting."

He bit down on his lip and looked down, and she started to smile, before quickly wiping the expression away.

"William, have you seen my mobile? It's not in any of my bags."

His gaze caught hers again. "Ah. That explains the mess. As a matter of fact, yes. I have it."

"Oh, thank goodness. Could I have it back, please?"

"Not quite yet."

She blinked. "I beg your pardon?"

He had the grace to look uncomfortable. "Look, Gabriella, the last thing we need is for you to post on your social media or something. Our PR department is looking after this. Our job is to lie low for a few days while they control the messaging. That means not being online."

Gabi clenched her fists as she stared at William. How had she ever thought him the fun brother? Stephen was somber but he wasn't stuffy or bossy. But William…this was infuriating! Who did he think he was?

"Then tell me that. Do not confiscate my phone like I am a disobedient child. I demand you give it back to me."

"So you can text your sister or parents? Do you have any idea how leaks happen?" He ran his hand over his hair. "I like your sister very much. She seems like a sweet girl. But she could get your family out of its financial bind by selling this story to the tabloids."

Gabi's mouth dropped open for a solid five seconds. And when she spoke again, her voice trembled with barely contained outrage.

"I don't know how your family does things, but that would never happen. I would trust Giulia with my life."

"And yet you didn't trust her with the truth yesterday."

Gabi sat heavily on the bed, the fight gone

out of her, at least for the moment. Deep down, she didn't blame William for being cautious. She had given him no reason to trust her. And yet… this was a most uncomfortable situation. Why should the two of them be at odds? They could work as a team, couldn't they? It didn't have to be a battle *royale*.

William finally moved from his spot by the door and came further into the room. He pulled up a small footstool and sat on it in front of her, resting his elbows on his knees. "I'm sorry," he said on a sigh. "I know I'm being harsh. I just…"

He sighed again, and Gabi got the feeling he wanted to say something but was holding off. "You just what?"

"I would do anything to protect Stephen. And that means this going to plan. He's been through enough."

"If you mean his relationship to Bridget…"

Hazel eyes caught hers and his mouth thinned. "You know."

"Of course I do." She kept her voice soft and even. "Stephen and I are friends, you know. At least we were. Until I panicked."

"Are you prone to panic?"

"Not really. I'm not prone to lying, either, so yesterday was a choice. I could lie to the world, but then I'd be lying to myself, too. And I couldn't live with that. So I panicked and I ran. I'm not proud of it, but here we are."

"Indeed."

"You're very loyal to your brother."

"I owe him a great deal." He smiled faintly. "I was on my way to being a big disappointment when he stepped in. I literally owe him my life. So yeah…you being angry that I took your phone isn't really going to shake me that much."

She should be mad, but the way he spoke about Stephen was so moving she couldn't hold on to her anger. She had no idea what Stephen had done, but clearly it was something huge. All the knowledge did was make her feel worse about what she'd done. Stephen hadn't deserved any of it. She should have spoken up sooner.

Except there'd been the afternoon when they'd walked around the Baresi villa, soaking in the sun. He'd told her then about his parents' love story, about how his father's death had affected them all, about how the indomitable Aurora Germain Pemberton was grieving. He'd been grieving, too, so much. As a friend, it was hard to refuse him comfort in that moment. A few weeks later he'd visited her in Italy and had presented her with his plan.

She looked at William and compared him to his brother. He wasn't quite as imposing as Stephen, but there was a strength about him that was reassuring as well as being infuriating. He'd lost his father, too. And he'd had his own grief to deal with. Maybe not the same pressures as Stephen, who was the eldest and the heir. But grief and adjustment all the same.

"I'm sorry," she said quietly now. "I'm sorry about your father. It must have been hard for you as well."

His eyes softened with sadness and pain. "He was a good man. Losing him was unexpected. We all managed to step into new roles in the company with only a few bumps. But living without him…that's different. So many times I've wanted to call him and ask his advice, and I can't."

"But Stephen's been the one in the spotlight. I hope you and your siblings haven't been forgotten."

He smiled a little. "Forgotten by the press? That's a blessing."

Of course. And if anyone found out they were here together, he'd be in the press and…it explained why he was holding on to her phone.

"Compromise?" she offered, her voice deliberately light. "You let me check my phone. You can vet any messages I send. And I will give it back to you. You trust me a little, and I'll trust you."

He considered for a moment, his gaze holding hers. Something strange swirled through her belly at his close examination. It was as if he could see right into her and her thoughts and feelings. She didn't really trust him at all. It was something he'd have to earn. But this might be a start.

He reached inside the back pocket of his jeans and pulled out her phone.

"You had it with you the whole time?" Gabi couldn't help the censure that colored her words.

And then he smiled. Smiled for the first time all morning. Had he smiled at all yesterday? She was hard-pressed to remember. But this one... oh, that swirly feeling came back with a vengeance. It lit up his face and made his eyes sparkle with impishness. Wasn't this inconvenient? The last thing she needed was to find her ex-fiancé's brother attractive.

"Of course I had it with me. And I was going to suggest what you just did. I don't want you to be a prisoner, Gabi. I just want this whole thing to be done cautiously and correctly."

"To protect Stephen."

"And the family. The tabloids will jump on any little thing, and while my mother is as strong as they come, I'd like to keep her from salacious speculation."

"You're very loyal," Gabi murmured, impressed despite herself.

"I protect people I care about," he admitted. "I didn't always, but I do now."

"In addition to managing part of the family business."

"That, too. It's been a big learning curve."

He handed her the phone and she cradled it in her hand. It was warm from being in his pocket and the knowledge felt more intimate than it should. "Thank you."

"After that, you're welcome to explore the château and the gardens. Just please don't leave the immediate property. As far as I know, no one knows we're here."

On one hand it was lovely to know she wouldn't be cooped up in the house. On the other, closeting her away felt strange and wrong. But it was only for a few days. That was what William had said.

And William, she was quickly realizing, appeared to be a man of his word. So far.

CHAPTER THREE

WILL PRESSED THE phone to his ear and closed his eyes. "Yes, I know. No one knows we're here, Stephen."

His brother went off again, and Will told himself to be patient. He understood Stephen being upset. He'd been betrayed, and if the truth got out, he'd be utterly humiliated. This wasn't the first time. Being rich and an earl made him desirable. But he was also very human, and right now his pride was understandably smarting. He'd never truly gotten over Bridget's betrayal. That was driving his emotion now more than Gabi, so William took a breath and stayed calm.

When Will could finally get a word in, he interrupted. "You should know that she's very contrite. She panicked. She didn't do this to create problems for you."

Why he was defending Gabi was a mystery. Maybe it was the soft look in her eyes this morning. Or how she'd offered a compromise and had stuck to it, no tantrums or pouting or trying to renegotiate. He pinched the skin above his nose and sighed. "Stephen, it was a stupid idea in the first place. And if you think she was using you, perhaps you need to look in the mirror. You were using her, too."

There was silence on the other end.

And then a click.

The beginning of a headache began behind his eyes now. Great. Stephen was mad, and Will didn't like that they were at odds. Meanwhile, he was stuck in France babysitting Gabi. Truthfully, that wasn't much of a hardship. She was rather lovely. Stephen would remember that when he got past his hurt pride.

He tucked the phone into his back pocket and stared out the window of his bedroom. There was very little of himself here; the rooms were professionally decorated and he'd always stayed in this room when they were in residence. His flat in Paris was much more his style. And yet he had to admit the light-colored walls and airy draperies contributed to the overall atmosphere of Château Germain: restful and calm.

The windows overlooked the terrace gardens, and always gave him a measure of peace. At twenty-eight, he was young to be in charge of an actual division of Aurora, and at times he wondered if it was what he really wanted. But there'd never been any question that he'd be part of the business, just like all the Germain-Pemberton children. His mother had put him at the helm of the fashion side of the business six months ago, which still struck him as humorous. But as she pointed out, he didn't need to know fashion to know business.

And what he knew was that Aurora, Inc., would never compromise on quality. The Baresi family had been their supplier for cashmere for nearly two decades. It was in Aurora's best interest to maintain that relationship.

How convenient that a member of the Baresi family was under the same roof.

A movement caught his eye, and he discovered Gabi walking through the terraced garden that led to the larger park beyond. His throat constricted as he tried to swallow. She wore the same dress she'd had on this morning, something simple with blue flowers on a white background, in a cut that emphasized her trim figure. But what really got his attention was her hair. This morning she'd been just out of the shower and it had been wound up in some sort of knot. But now it flowed down past her shoulders, a curtain of rich mink, thick and wavy. The kind of hair a man itched to sink his fingers into. He imagined doing so and hearing her sigh with pleasure…

But Gabi was not for him. He wouldn't do that to Stephen. Besides, they were all trying to avoid a scandal here.

She stopped by a rosebush and he caught himself smiling as she leaned forward to smell a blossom. Could he be more of a fool?

He wiped the smile from his face and decided to join her in the garden. There was no reason why she couldn't have what she wanted. A deeper alliance with Baresi was a solid business move for Aurora. Stephen had attached conditions to his offer. William would, too, but it wouldn't require anyone to sacrifice their principles or integrity. He'd do this for the company, and for Baresi, and let Stephen worry about procreating and providing an heir and a baby for their mother to bounce on her knee.

The garden reminded Gabi of home.

Provençal climate meant many of the plants, shrubs and flowers were of the Mediterranean variety, and very unlike the English garden back at Chatsworth Hall. Boxwoods, olive trees and cypress flanked flower and herb gardens that cascaded down each terrace. The smell was incredible. She was sure she sensed the tart aroma of lemons and perhaps the softer scent of nectarine…was there an orchard somewhere on the grounds? In the garden proper there was rosemary and thyme and of course lavender, the savory scents soothing her frayed nerves as she made her way to the gurgling fountain in the very center.

The fountain was a little oasis, with a few

Aleppo pines providing a bit of shade and wicker furniture placed around it for a wanderer to take a moment to rest. She did, easing herself into a chair with a creak. It was exceedingly comfortable, and Gabi let out a long, slow breath. Her anxiety had been on high alert for hours. She needed to decompress, so she focused on breathing, checking in with each of her senses.

The feel of the chair, beneath her bottom, the armrests beneath her fingers, warm and dry and textured. The perfumed, soft air. The way the light breeze fluttered nearby leaves ever so gently, a susurrus of sound that shivered along her nerve endings, inviting her to relax. The sun on her face, and William, walking down the terrace with long-legged grace.

William!

So much for relaxing. She'd already agonized over her reaction to him this morning. Up until two months ago, she hadn't even met Stephen's brother. At the time she remembered thinking how handsome looks ran in the family, but she'd been so distracted by her father's test results and Stephen's proposition that he'd been relegated to the background.

He wasn't in the background now, and she still hadn't figured out how to handle him. Or if she even should try.

She reminded herself to relax her muscles, so that when he arrived by her side, she looked for all the world as if she were enjoying a sunny afternoon in a spectacular garden.

"I see you discovered the gardens. They're lovely, aren't they?"

"Some of it reminds me of home," she replied, smiling up at him. "But the lavender…it weaves its way through everything, doesn't it?"

"You can't see them, but there are fields nearby. And we always have some in the gardens."

"It's supposed to be good for anxiety." She laughed lightly. "My own little aromatherapy afternoon."

He looked over his shoulder and then back at her again. "If you need help relaxing, I did ask for some wine to be brought out. I'd like to talk to you about something."

Unease centered in her gut. So far, William had been honest, telling her exactly what was on his mind. She respected that. She could deal with that. She couldn't deal with half-truths and angles and trying to pretty something up that was downright ugly. She'd been through enough of that already. She'd been willing to agree to Stephen's offer because Luca had strung her along for two years before shattering her dreams. She wanted marriage and a family. Stephen had offered both. Luca, on the other hand, already had a wife. A wife she'd known nothing about until she'd had her own pregnancy scare. Then the truth had come out. Luca had broken her heart and made her feel stupid in equal measure.

But she also reminded herself that Will had his own agenda, which was about what was good for Aurora, Inc. She forgot that at her peril.

"All right." She sat up straighter, encouraged when William grabbed a nearby chair and pulled it over closer to her. At least he wasn't going to stand over her in a very obvious position of power. Power which, of course, he had. She'd lost her only bargaining chip to save her family.

A maid approached, carrying a tray with wine-glasses and a chilled bottle. With a small smile she set the tray on the little table. William nodded and smiled at her. "Thank you, Angeline. I can pour for us."

Gabi had no doubt the wine would be excellent, and she was of two minds about the motivation behind it. William might be trying to broach his topic in a convivial manner. Or he might be lulling her into thinking that, using it to his advantage. Either way, she was on her guard.

He handed her the glass, touched the rim with his own and said a quiet, "Cheers."

She sipped, enjoying the taste of the liquid on her tongue. *"Grazie,"* she said softly. "It's very good."

"You don't speak Italian much."

She smiled. "I do when I'm angry. And with family. But business…that's mostly in English."

"You've been working for the family business for some time now."

She sipped again, and then casually responded, "As have you."

"Did you always want to?"

How could she answer that? Truthfully, no. She hadn't grown up with this burning desire to take over her father's business. In fact, the agreement with Stephen had benefited her as well as her father. With Baresi under the Aurora, Inc., umbrella, she would have been free to move on once their marriage ended, if she wanted to. Now she was going to be responsible for the company whether she liked it or not.

She shifted uncomfortably.

"It's a big world," she finally answered. "But I also love my family and it's a good job."

"But not your calling."

She sighed. "You're talking about something different, a vocation, yes? A higher purpose?" A frown tipped her lips downward. "I don't know. Running the company has never been a driving force for me."

"If you could do anything, what would it be?"

She met his gaze. "I don't know. I figured that if I found it, I'd know."

He nodded, his brows pulling together. "I think we might be more similar than we thought," he murmured. "Both of us love our families. We're in the family business. And yet we wonder if there's something more."

"There's not for me, not right now, and that's okay." She figured she might as well be honest, just in case Stephen hadn't given him all the particulars. "My papa…he's very ill. The doctors say the survival rate is promising, but the treatments…without him, Baresi can't survive. He *is* Baresi. Now that I've messed everything up, I'm going to have to go home once this PR nightmare is over and do my best to keep it alive until he returns." She swallowed against the lump in her throat. She refused to think the words *if he returns.*

William's keen gaze locked on her face. "Maybe that's a way to ease out of the engagement publicly. Say that you've returned home to care for the family business while your father is ill."

"It would tie it up neatly, but no. I'm not using my papa as a…what's the word? A scapegoat."

His eyes glowed. "Damn, Gabi. That made me like you a little bit."

She laughed in response, because it was so unexpected. "You didn't like me before?"

"I didn't know you. I just had impressions and what Stephen told me. But I'm forming my own opinion. As much as you've landed us in this mess, I cannot argue with your principles." His lips turned up in a smile. "Just your timing."

"I'm so glad my principles measure up," she replied. And took a healthy sip of wine, because the twinkle in William's eyes made her think they had somehow made the switch to flirting. How could she be doing that a mere twenty-four hours after fleeing the Chatsworth chapel? And when they didn't trust each other?

His phone buzzed and she watched as he leaned forward and removed it from his pocket, then swiped his finger over the screen to unlock it. His smile turned to a frown and he sighed. "I asked my assistant to keep me updated on what's happening online."

He handed her the phone so she could see. His assistant, whoever she was, had included links. So many that Gabi had to scroll with her finger—twice—to see them all.

"So many," she whispered.

"It'll go from here to some of the tabloids by tomorrow, I think. And within a week or so it'll quiet. We have to outlast the news cycle, and not create a new one."

"It's a lot. But I'm a nobody. Why is anyone interested?"

"Because Stephen is an earl and because our mother is Aurora Germain. She's known all over the world."

"She must hate me right now."

"Not hate. My mother doesn't hate people. But I can guarantee she's not happy."

"Should I talk to her?" It was the last thing she wanted to do, but she'd been the one to make the mess. She should be the one to reach out. Even if the thought made her the teensiest bit sick to her stomach.

"Not now." He took the phone back and tucked it away. "Listen, look at this week as a vacation. The château is lovely and you have the run of it and the gardens. The library is packed with books. There's a theater room with a huge movie selection. This'll be over before you know it."

And she'd be bored to tears. But as consequences went, she couldn't complain. There were so many worse things than boredom.

So why did she feel like crying all of a sudden?

She looked away and sniffed, tried to keep her lower lip from wobbling. She wasn't a crier and she definitely didn't want to lose her grip in front of William, especially since she'd broken down briefly yesterday. And yet somehow the urge would not go away. A tear trembled on her lashes and snuck down her cheek.

"Gabi?" His voice was hesitant, surprised. "What's wrong?"

How could she explain? There were so many emotions roiling around inside her she didn't know where to start.

She sniffed again, but it was no use. Now that she'd started, she had the feeling she was going to have to cry it out and get it out of her system.

"What is it?" he said gently, and he put his hand over hers on the wicker armrest.

His fingers were warm and strong as they enveloped hers, and another emotion bloomed in her chest, adding on to the complicated feelings she was already battling. Oh, he shouldn't be nice to her. This wouldn't do at all. She had to keep the wall between them standing strong.

"I'm fine," she tried, and sniffed again. Why wouldn't her nose stop running?

He took his hand away, much to her relief, but it was short-lived as a moment later he held out a handkerchief.

She dabbed her eyes and nose and laughed a little. "Seriously? I didn't think men carried these anymore."

"Maman always insisted we have one for emergencies. It stuck. Comes in handy for damsels in distress, too."

She dabbed again and met his gaze. Her eyes must be red now and the tip of her nose, too, but she didn't care. "Despite all appearances to the contrary, I do not need to be rescued."

"Good. I'm glad." He put his hands on his knees. "It means you're made of strong stuff. Stiff upper lip and all that."

She chuckled. He sounded so perfectly English in that moment.

"Here," he suggested, and topped up her glass. "Take an hour and let yourself feel what you need to. Drink wine. Soak in the garden. I'm sure you've got some thinking to do. And when you're ready, come find me. We can talk about what comes next."

He got up from the chair and prepared to leave.

"William?"

"Hmm?"

"Why are you being so nice to me?"

His hazel gaze locked with hers, and that strange feeling came over her again. Ugh! If only she could have felt like this when Stephen looked at her, she wouldn't be in this predicament!

"Because being a jerk rarely accomplishes anything. And because you nearly went through with a fake marriage to save your family. That's brave. So was walking away from it. Don't get me wrong, I was furious yesterday. It's a hell of a mess to try to control, but I don't think you did it maliciously. You've got a strong character, Gabi, and I respect that a lot."

She was pretty sure her mouth was hanging open at this point. "I…thank you. I don't really know how to respond to that. Except that I'm so glad you understand why I did what I did. I'm so sorry I've caused so much trouble."

"Stephen bears some of the blame, too," William replied. "And I've told him so. He didn't like it."

She laughed again despite herself. "No, he wouldn't. He's stubborn." She sighed. "I've probably ruined any friendship we had. I regret that. Your brother is a very good man. There just weren't any—"

She stopped abruptly. There was no way she was going to talk about sexual attraction with William. Not considering the way her pulse leaped every time he appeared.

"Sparks? Fireworks?" he filled in for her.

Her cheeks, which she imagined were already pink from crying, heated.

William laughed, presumably at her discomfiture. "No need to be shy now. And to be honest, I'm kind of glad to hear it." He stepped away. "Enjoy your afternoon, Gabi."

He turned and walked back on the cobbles, his shoes echoing through the peaceful afternoon. She watched him go, let out a breath that she hoped would calm the beating of her heart. What had he meant just now, that he was glad to hear it?

Why would he be happy there'd never been any chemistry between her and his brother?

CHAPTER FOUR

By Wednesday, Gabi was going crazy. She'd read three books, watched two movies, wandered the gardens, slept, ate delicious food and drank excellent wine. For the first day, it was lovely—as William had said, it was a vacation of sorts. And who didn't want that? But on Tuesday she'd found herself restless. And by Wednesday afternoon, she was ready for a change of scenery. Not that the château staff wasn't lovely; they were. But she'd hardly seen William, either. Once a day they had a meal together, but he spent a lot of time in a downstairs office, working remotely.

While she had no purpose at all beyond staying out of sight. And presumably out of mind, too.

This morning she'd popped down to the kitchens to ask a favor, since she wasn't allowed to go into the nearby town. She'd given a simple shopping list to the cook and now she was heading downstairs to whip up her own dinner. She needed to do something with her hands and to keep her mind occupied, and cooking was just the thing. She needed a taste of...home.

She was homesick. She missed her apartment in Perugia, family meals at the villa, even the Baresi offices where she did most of her work. But most of all she missed Mama and Papa, and their ready smiles and hugs. Right now her papa was preparing for surgery followed by chemotherapy. And she was stuck here, unable to go to him or even tell him what was happening. She was lying. And if anything happened to him and the lie stood between them...

The kitchen was quiet when she entered, and she found the ingredients she'd asked for in the massive refrigerator. Before she began, she opened the bottle of wine that she'd placed in the fridge earlier. Since William had said she could have full run of the château, she'd made a trip to the wine cellar and had been delighted to find an Orvieto that looked to do the trick. A little taste of home.

The first thing she did was put an apron on over her jeans and top. Even though she'd dressed casually, her first job had the potential to be a messy one. She rinsed the cherries and put them in a bowl, and then went to work pitting and slicing them in half. Juice stained her fingers and now and then one of the cherries would squirt as she removed the pit. She popped one in her mouth at the end, then put red wine, sugar and orange zest in a pan to heat. Poached cherries was one of her favorite desserts growing up, and so very simple to make.

Once that was on the go and set aside, she turned to her vegetables.

Vignole was something she remembered from childhood, particularly when spring came and everything was fresh and new. The tension started to unwind in Gabi's body as she prepared the artichokes, leeks, peas and fava beans. Garlic and onion went into the pot, and broth, and then the artichokes.

There would be far more than she would be able to eat, but she didn't care. This felt right. And it felt, in some small way, like something she could control when everything else was out of control. She raised her glass in a toast to herself and took a long, revivifying drink.

As everything bubbled and aromas rose in the air around her, she drizzled honey into a bowl of mascarpone, to go on top of the cherries. Her mouth watered just thinking about it.

"Hullo! Madame Gosselin…" Gabi turned as William entered the kitchen, releasing a torrent of French that she didn't understand.

"Oh," he said, breaking off midsentence and staring. "I didn't know you were in here. I was looking for Madame Gosselin."

"She gave me use of her kitchen," Gabi said softly.

"I see that. You cook."

"Of course. If I didn't cook, I'd starve." She laughed a little. "I needed something to do, and I was missing home and my mama's cooking. So here I am."

He relaxed and came farther into the kitchen. "What are you making? It smells amazing."

"*Vignole*—it's a vegetable stew. Nothing heavy. Lots of vegetables and broth and a little pancetta. There's fresh bread from this morning."

He leaned over the pot and inhaled the steam. "Mmm. And what's in here?"

She reached for the copper pot and took it off the burner. "Poached cherries to serve with a bowl of mascarpone cream for dessert."

"A feast," he said, and smiled at her.

Oh, no. Not the smile again. This was why it was good he'd hidden away in the office for the past few days. Every time he smiled at her she forgot who she was for a brief second, and who he was, and why this was so very inadvisable. If a runaway bride was a mess, this situation would be catastrophic.

So it made absolutely no sense that she smiled in return and said, "There's plenty for both of us, if you'd like dinner."

"I'd like that. Don't tell Madame Gosselin, but my tastes are a little more simple than what she puts together."

"Surely you had your share of French food

growing up." She waved a hand, gesturing to nothing in particular in the kitchen. "Between here and Paris."

"Yes, but I also lived in England a good part of the year. And the family has properties all over."

She stirred the stew and he came up behind her and looked over her shoulder into the pot. She was startled at having him so near; she could smell his cologne and the lighter fragrance in his hair from his shampoo. Unsettled, she moved away so she could slice the bread.

"So what's your favorite meal in the world?" he asked. "If you could have absolutely anything?"

She thought for a moment, her hand paused on the bread loaf. "There's a restaurant in Perugia that I adore. My parents took me there for my eighteenth birthday and now I go every year. They make the most amazing pasta with a butter truffle sauce. Every time I go I swear I'm going to have something different, but then… I always go back to it."

"Mmm…sounds delicious."

"What's yours?"

"When I was in uni, there was a curry takeaway just around the corner from our flat. I'd eat anything from there any day of the week." He frowned. "I don't even know if it's still there."

"You should go back and find out." She

grinned at him and put down the knife. "And you surprise me. I expected something elaborate and fancy."

"Not me. If I can't have that, I'll take a traditional English breakfast all the way. I get that from my father."

"You miss him." She'd been reaching for the olive oil, but she hesitated and met his gaze evenly. "I really am sorry."

"None of us expected it. He was only in his early sixties, you know? He should have had more time."

She swallowed thickly. At twenty-eight, she was the oldest. Giulia was only twenty-one. Her father was only fifty-four. What if he didn't make it? She bit down on her lip and remained silent.

"You said your father's prognosis is good. You need to hold on to that."

It surprised her that he'd guessed the path of her thoughts. "I know, but there's always that other number that sneaks up and reminds you that not everyone is lucky. The business aside, I don't know what we'd do without him."

William came around the table where she was working and took her hands. "When is his surgery?"

"Next week. Stephen and I were going to stop for a few days on our way home from Malta, but now…" She tried not to think about him touching her, but her fingers tingled from the contact. Oh, this would not do at all...

A strong finger tilted up her chin. "Now you're not in Malta. But I'll do what I can to get you home so you can be there, for him and for your family. Will you let me arrange it?"

That he even offered filled her heart with joy and relief. "Oh, William, that means so much to me. If I can be home when he has his operation..." She took his hand in hers. "When can I tell Mama?"

His eyes clouded a bit. "Not yet. I don't want to set something in stone until the rest of the week plays out. Can you trust me? And not because you don't have a choice, but because you know I'll do my best?"

She wanted to trust him, and that scared her to bits. Look at what had happened the last time she trusted someone. Maybe the problem wasn't with trusting others, maybe it was trusting herself. Because twice now she'd landed in "relationships" that were nothing but lies.

"You haven't given me a reason not to. Yet."

"I'll endeavor to keep your good opinion of me," he said formally, and it made her smile again.

"Come on, then. I think this is ready, and you can eat a very Umbrian dish tonight instead of Madame Gosselin's heavy sauces."

"Music to my ears," he said, and went to find bowls and plates.

* * *

Will looked across the table at Gabi and knew he was asking for trouble.

The candlelight lit her face, and when she laughed it was like music. The meal she'd prepared had been fairly simple but amazingly delicious. For dessert, he'd headed to the basement for an appropriate wine. Not a dessert wine, but a red that would complement the cherries and also be drinkable throughout the evening.

Right now Gabi was pushing her remaining cherries around her bowl with a spoon. "Full?" he asked, dipping his own spoon for one more scrumptious bite.

"Very. Madame Gosselin really knows how to bake bread."

"Once, when we were kids, Charlotte and I snuck into the kitchen at night and toasted a whole loaf. We spread it with Nutella and nearly made ourselves sick. The next morning there were chocolate fingerprints on everything."

She laughed, a light, lovely sound. How had Stephen thought he could marry her and not fall in love with her? What was wrong with him?

"Your mother had her hands full with twins."

"Yes. And you know, despite being 'the' Aurora of Aurora, Inc., she spent a lot of time parenting us. Both our parents did. We had a nanny, but we were never made to be out of the way. We were…are…a family."

"I like your mother. She frightens me, but she's lovely just the same. She has this aura about her that is so strong and capable."

"She is," William agreed. "But she has her weaknesses, too. No," he corrected, "not weaknesses. Love is not a weakness. She has a wonderful soft side. I think that's why Stephen felt so pressured to marry. After he broke with Bridget, Maman was devastated. She'd put a lot of hope into that relationship. It's horrible seeing your very strong and capable mother reduced by grief. It was like she'd lost her husband and then the family hope for the future, too."

There. He'd brought Stephen back into the conversation. That should help steer his thoughts away from where they shouldn't be. On Gabi and her smooth skin and gorgeous hair and musical laugh.

Gabi reached for her wine, sat back, took a drink and licked her lips. And Stephen was quickly forgotten.

"I should go do the dishes," Gabi said, a little reluctantly. "Confession. I love to cook. Hate cleaning up."

"I'll help. It's the least I can do since you fed me."

They stacked their dishes and made their way to the kitchen again, but when they arrived it was sparkling clean and one of the maids was putting away the copper pots.

"Oh! We were just coming to tidy!"

The maid smiled and replied in French. William said a quick *merci* and *bonne nuit* and then put down their dishes and guided Gabi out of the kitchen. "What did she say?" she asked.

"She said it was no trouble and that if we left the dishes she'd put them in the dishwasher."

"Oh. I'm not used to that."

"Now you're free to enjoy the evening." Which he guessed would be without him, and he knew it should be even as he hoped it would not.

She sighed. "I'll confess, I've had my fill of peace and quiet. I wish I could go and *do* something." She turned her gaze up to his. "But I understand why I cannot. I don't mean to complain. I know I brought this on myself."

Will thought for a few minutes. So far, their PR strategy had worked perfectly. They'd leaked a few lines about Gabi being ill, recuperating at Chatsworth, and despite gossip to the contrary, they'd set a bogus new tentative date for the wedding. It looked as if there was no trouble in paradise as far as communications from Aurora went. Soon there would be another story with different celebs, and this delicious little tidbit would be mostly forgotten. Taking her back to Chatsworth wasn't possible; she wasn't exactly welcome there and he understood why. But if he took her home to Italy next week, he could probably leave her there, safe with her family. And temptation would be firmly out of his way.

Which did nothing about her boredom this evening.

"We could take a walk in the lemon grove," he suggested, suddenly inspired. "I know I've insisted you stay in the garden, but I don't think anyone suspects you're here. It's a gorgeous night. I know it's not a night on the town, but it's better than nothing."

"I'd like that."

The day's heat held in the air as they left the château through the garden. The sun was retreating but the moon wasn't out yet, and the sky was a soft blend of blues and pale pinks announcing the beginning of sunset. A smear of cloud carried the colors across the horizon, and William took a deep breath. There was something so different in the air here, as distinctive as terroir to a grape. It was the combination of earthiness, the proximity to the Mediterranean, the vegetation and, for lack of a better word, the utter *Frenchness* of it all. Tonight there was nowhere else he'd rather be than walking through the stone gate from the olive-bordered gardens to the orchard beyond, where the leafy trees provided a shadowy canopy as they ambled along.

"Better?" he asked, breaking the silence.

"Much. What trees are in here?"

"Oh, lemons, and some oranges, and over in that corner are some nectarines."

"Was it ever farmed?"

"Maybe? I don't know for sure. My parents bought this place when I was very little. It hasn't been in the family that long, you know?" He shrugged. "We have a gardener. He cares for the groves now and picks the fruit."

"And the lavender?" She stopped and pointed over the hill to the sloping purple fields below. "Do you own those fields as well?"

"No. But we source it for our fragrances. However, that is not my department. I'm trying to learn more about fabrics and fashion these days."

"Like cashmere."

"Exactly."

"In that case, let me help." She grinned up at him. "You can't find better than Baresi."

He paused for a moment, wondering if now was the right time to broach the topic. Gabi could have thrown a tantrum about this week. She could have made things difficult. Instead she'd done everything he'd asked in order to minimize the damage to his family, even knowing that the chance of saving hers was gone.

Except it wasn't.

The twilight deepened and he reached for her hand. "Come with me for a moment. I want to talk to you about something."

There was an old bench down the path, almost

forgotten among the grass and shrubs. But William knew it was there. He knew because when he was fourteen he'd spied on his sister one day when she'd gone walking with a boy and they'd sat on the bench to kiss. Charlotte had given him half her pocket money for the holiday to keep him from telling their father.

Now he sat on it with his brother's ex-fiancée. He wondered what price Charlotte would demand if she knew, and he laughed a little.

"What's so funny?" Gabi sat beside him and tilted her head a little.

"I was remembering something from my childhood. It involved my sister, a local boy and extortion."

"Oh, my." A warm smile bloomed on her face. "I love stories like that. Those are the kinds of shared family memories that last, aren't they? I hope you weren't too demanding."

"Half of her allowance for the six weeks we were here. I spent it unwisely and it was the most fun I've ever had."

"Poor Charlotte. She's too sweet for that."

"Don't let her fool you."

They sat for a moment and then, when the silence drew out, Gabi said, "What did you want to talk to me about?"

He turned on the bench so he was facing her. "This business agreement with Baresi… I know Stephen set it up as a mutually beneficial arrangement. But the thing is… I think it's mutually beneficial, even without the marriage. I've looked at our history with Baresi. I've looked at the quality. There's no reason we can't enter into some sort of agreement that benefits us both." He held her gaze. "Without you having to marry someone you don't love."

Her cheeks pinkened. "But…" The word trailed away. He could see the question in her face, though, and he didn't have a good answer.

"I don't know why Stephen wouldn't have just made the deal. Maybe it was pressure from our mother—she can be very persuasive. Or his way of dealing with his own broken heart—to give it to someone where it would be safe from harm." He met her gaze steadily. "If you're not in love, you're safe from having your heart broken."

"That seems a bit poetic for Stephen."

"Maybe. I can't speak to my brother's motives, but truthfully…in my opinion this would be a sound deal, period. There's no reason why we can't partner with you. It gives us a steady supply of top-quality material, and to be honest, it would elevate Baresi's status in the industry."

She stared at him. "I didn't have to marry him."

"No. And he shouldn't have asked it of you. I love my brother, Gabi. I'll do what I can to protect him, always. But that doesn't mean I agree with all his actions, and in this he was wrong."

There was one sticking point, and he felt duty-bound to bring it up. "It's not a sure thing yet. I'm head of the division, but Stephen is head of acquisitions. He'll have to approve it."

He watched carefully as her face fell. She tried to hide her disappointment, but it was impossible. "And he hates me right now."

"*Hate* is a strong word. Besides, I'm positive that he's going to come to the conclusion that you saved him from a very big mistake. Let me handle Stephen. You worry about your family."

Her eyes widened as she reached out and touched his hand. "Why are you doing this for me? Why aren't you as mad as Stephen?"

She was so beautiful in the fading light. Her eyes were soft velvet, her skin luminous. He couldn't remember another woman capturing his attention this way, which complicated everything. He had to keep this just business, and when she looked into his eyes like she was right now, it was impossible to think in terms of dollars and cents. Yes, getting her back to Italy and leaving her there was a very good idea. Out of sight, out of mind.

"I wasn't the groom, Gabi. My pride wasn't crushed. I was called in to do damage control."

"I know. It just baffles me." She looked away. "You should be angry. I deserve for you to be angry."

"No, not angry. Look at it this way. If I had

the chance to make things right and maybe save *my* father, I'd do it. I can't save him now. My father is gone. But yours isn't. Why wouldn't I want to help?"

Her eyes misted over as she looked back at him and squeezed his hand. "You're a good man, William Pemberton. Better than I realized."

"We barely knew each other before Saturday night," he observed, keeping his voice light, but the compliment struck him right in the heart. If he was a good man it was because of his brother's support and his father's patience. He tried to remember that every day and let it guide his actions. His days of making messes were over. Now he tried to clean them up. Be someone his family could depend on. That person he was before could never be resurrected. He looked at Gabi, so forbidden to him, so beautiful. She could make him forget for a few moments, and that was dangerous.

"We should probably get back," she said quietly after a few minutes of silence. The air was soft and the world around them seemed colored in muted pinks and periwinkle as the sun slid closer to the horizon. It was the time of day for whispered secrets and hidden smiles, forbidden touches and soft sighs. That in between time when possibilities were waiting to be plucked like fruit from the tree, and romance bloomed around every corner.

Their gazes held, and for the space of a held breath, they drifted close together. His heart pounded as his gaze dropped to her ripe lips. And then William broke the spell and stood abruptly.

"You're right. We should get back. I want to start drafting a proposal and also work on travel arrangements."

Gabi's face shifted back to impersonal and friendly, thank goodness. He wasn't sure he had the strength to resist her if she'd pushed their... intimacy. Was that what it was? This feeling that kept coming over him? She felt it, too, didn't she? All the more reason to keep his distance now and get her back to Italy as soon as feasible.

"Of course," she answered, also rising. She started back along the rows of the lemon trees, toward the château towering in the distance.

Maybe it had been a mistake bringing her here. William had only been thinking of privacy and seclusion. He hadn't thought of the unintended consequences of being here together, yet alone.

They could be friendly. And friends. But anything more was impossible. He could never betray Stephen that way. Even if his brother wasn't in love with Gabi, it would be wrong, wouldn't it? Besides, if a runaway bride was a PR nightmare for Aurora, imagine what would follow if William suddenly showed up with her on his arm?

"You go on ahead. I'm going to...check on something." He knew he sounded lame, but walking through the gardens and into the château together meant separating there and he wanted to kiss her so badly he could nearly taste her lips just from the mere thought.

"Thank you for the walk. And letting me get out a bit more."

"Thank you for dinner," he replied, and then made a turn on the path and headed in a different direction.

It was the best way. It was the only way.

CHAPTER FIVE

THE WALK IN the garden had been a mistake.

For the first time since her arrival, William had given her access to a laptop. "You need to see what's happened," he'd said, his voice brittle. He hadn't shown her any tabloid links since that first day. Now, though, he'd given her full access. "I trust you won't make this worse by responding to anything." There'd been barely concealed anger in his tone. "This wasn't your fault. It was mine. I should have anticipated this would happen."

But she stared at the picture and knew she wasn't blameless. How could she be? A photog's massive lens had done its job. Their identities were clear as they sat on the stone bench. And so was the fact that her hand was on his and they were gazing at each other dreamily. She could pass it off and say it was nothing more than gratitude, but she'd be wrong. She liked William, a lot. And that walk had been ridiculously romantic.

She muttered a stream of words in Italian that

she hoped William couldn't translate. He was on the other side of the room, talking on his cell, but his eyes never left her. Flat. Assessing. Because now she'd become another problem that needed solving.

For the first time since arriving, she got angry. Angry at Stephen for suggesting their crazy arrangement. Angry that he could have helped her without coercing her to marry him. And really, truly angry at herself for going along with it, and not being stronger in the face of her own personal crises. That was really why they were in this mess. It was up to her to get them out of this conundrum. She was done being a pawn in anyone's agenda. And she was done reacting out of fear and distress.

And yet her heart seized as she thought of Baresi Textiles. If she made a misstep, it could all go wrong and she could add to her father's burdens rather than solve them. But she had cards to play, didn't she? And she could use them. For a week she'd been docile and nice and sweet and full of self-blame. Where had the self-assured, proactive woman she'd worked so hard to become gone? She didn't like that when things went sideways, she'd made weak decisions. Well, no more. She was going to go home and she was going to handle the business until her father was well enough to come back.

She closed the browser, making the photo and

the accompanying headline disappear. The fact that the article asked if the wedding had been called off because she was "cavorting" with the groom's brother was too much.

It was time to go back to Perugia.

She rose from her chair and stood tall, then crossed the library to where William stood. "When you're done your call, I want to speak with you."

Then she turned and walked away. She was tired of doing everything on Pemberton terms. William had been kind, there was no doubt about that. And there were far worse things than spending a week in a château in Provence. But it hadn't actually solved anything. Her guilt over leaving Stephen at the altar had prompted her to go along with the plan. That guilt was diminishing by the day.

The important thing was to get through this so that Baresi ended up in a strong position. That was the only consideration now.

She went to her room, that lovely, airy, restful room, and got her suitcase out of the wardrobe. Then she started packing it, piece by piece, folding each item carefully, the exact opposite of what she'd done on her arrival. She looked at the garment bag holding the wedding dress and closed the door of the wardrobe. She would leave it behind. There was no use for it now, and it was nothing more than dead weight to carry around.

William knocked and she latched the wardrobe door before saying, "Come in."

He looked at the suitcase on the bed and his brows pulled together. "Going somewhere?"

"Home. This is ridiculous. I should have gone home in the first place. It's where I belong."

"I know this is a setback, but we're dealing with it."

She put her hands on her hips and let out a sigh. "William, I don't want to be something you have to 'deal with.' I did everything you asked without complaint for the better part of a week and it changed nothing. If anything, it made things worse." She tried to ignore the niggling fact that the press had picked up on some sort of attraction between them. One they wouldn't act on but that was there just the same.

"It's my fault. I suggested the walk. It had been quiet, and I didn't consider someone would be out there with a massive camera lens. I got careless."

"Would it be so bad if we told the truth? That I decided we didn't suit and took the blame?"

He gave his head a shake. "Are you serious? Then the story becomes all about what possible deficiencies Stephen has, since it clearly isn't his money or position."

Gabi spun away, frustrated beyond belief. "But they're going to spin it no matter what! So why can't we, I don't know, live our lives?" She turned back to face him. "Stephen is a big boy. Why do you have to handle everything?"

"Because I owe him," William shot back.

"Owe him for what?"

"Saving me from myself, all right?"

Silence fell over the room. Gabi wondered what in the world that meant.

"I understand family loyalty—"

"You have no idea," he interrupted. "I owe William, and my father, everything. I can never repay our dad. But I owe Stephen this. I'm no longer a mess to clean up, you see? I'm the one who does the cleaning up. That's how it is now."

She didn't even know what that meant. "Then we're right back where we started. I'm the mess. So let's take me out of the equation. I'll go back to Italy and my family. Completely out of your hair."

William ran his fingers through his hair. "Are you mad? You think they won't find you there, either?"

"So what's your brilliant idea? How are you going to control the story this time?" She raised her voice in frustration, and he did the same.

"I don't know, all right?"

Was it absolutely bonkers to feel like crossing the room to kiss him right now? What was wrong with her?

And then *he* did it. William took a half dozen

long strides, pulled her into his arms and pressed his mouth to hers.

There was a brief moment of surprise and then she wrapped her arms around him, sliding her fingers into the hair just above his neck. Excitement jangled from her belly up through her chest, catching her breath as she responded to the feel of his lips on hers. His arm settled at the hollow of her back and pulled her tightly against his hard body. Oh, *magnifico*. The word slipped into her brain on a sigh as her body ignited against his fit physique.

She nibbled on his lower lip and he moaned, then pushed her away and stood back, his chest rising and falling rapidly as he stared at her. His hair was slightly mussed and his lips swollen, and his jeans… She swallowed thickly. *Magnifico*, indeed. *Fantastico. Splendido.* And about a hundred other adjectives she could think of.

"That was a spectacular mistake," he ground out, his voice gritty with frustration.

Gabi straightened her shoulders and reminded herself to be calm, despite the crazy beating of her heart. "Oh? I'm glad we got it out of the way. It's been brewing all week. At least now I don't have to wonder."

"Wonder? What are you talking about?"

She tucked her hair behind her ears. "I got the feeling there was some chemistry between us. Then I wondered if I'd imagined it. Now I know."

"Chemistry!" he exploded.

In another situation she might have laughed at the astounded expression on his face, as if she'd said something both preposterous and unsavory. But this was a serious situation. It made the mess even more complicated.

"We ignore it at our peril," she advised, trying to sound logical. It was difficult, though, because he looked so utterly delicious and the taste of him was still on her lips. "That picture caught us in a vulnerable moment, Will. It looks bad because we *were* gazing at each other." She wiped a hand over her face. "It's annoying and problematic, but the worst thing we can do is pretend what just happened never happened."

His expression darkened. "Stephen is my brother." His voice was low and seemed to hold a warning.

"I know that."

"Less than a week ago, you were going to marry him."

"Thank you for the recap."

His eyes sparked, more green than hazel at the moment. "Stop that. You're being...troublesome."

"After last weekend? Also not news. And your finely executed plan didn't exactly work. Here I am in the tabloids again." She glared. "I trusted you and your precious plan, and look where it landed us. I won't make that mistake again."

He clamped his lips shut.

"I am going back to Italy. I'm going to be with my parents as my father prepares for surgery. And you're going to help me do it."

"You're hardly in a position to make demands," he shot back, shoving his hands in his pockets.

She took a moment to breathe, swallow and stand tall even though inside she was quivering. She lifted her chin and met his gaze. "I'm in a perfect position to make demands. Because if you don't, I'm sure the press would be interested in a few details from the past week."

Gabi hated the words immediately after saying them. Extortion wasn't her style, and neither was deliberately hurting someone. But William had to believe she'd follow through. It was the only way to regain control of the situation. The only way to go home. That was all she really wanted to do now. Be with her family. Get back to her life and start rebuilding.

"You wouldn't."

"I don't want to, but I would. I've played it your way and all it's done is keep me closeted away and bored for a week."

The green in his eyes dulled as he stared at her. "Gabriella."

"You're very displeased. You always call me Gabi."

"I thought we were becoming friends."

She huffed. "Don't try that, Will. Friends don't kiss like we just kissed. What am I to you? For-

bidden fruit? You don't want to betray your brother. I get that. Believe me, I understand family loyalty. And while running from my wedding does not demonstrate the best judgment, I'm really quite smart. It made sense for me to lie low for a few days. Now I need to start controlling the story instead of hiding from it."

"I don't like it." He moved to a chair and sat down with a sigh. "When you control it, it means I don't."

"Ah, yes." She smiled faintly and sat across from him. Now they were getting somewhere. "And you don't trust me. I don't blame you. I haven't given you much reason to. Except that I've followed your every instruction all week." She raised an eyebrow.

"You have," he admitted.

"I promise that if you let me return to my family now, I will keep to the original story. I fell ill and recovered for a few days, then took some quiet time at the family château. I'll frame it as you and I are friends, as we should be as future in-laws. I'll even hint at the new wedding date. But I'm not going to stay hidden away like a princess in a tower."

"I'm going with you."

"That will only fuel the rumors."

He ran a finger along his chin. "Too bad. That's my condition." He frowned, his brows pulling together. "In fact, what makes the most sense is for Stephen to meet us there."

Her head shot up in alarm. "Stephen? Whatever for?"

"Because you should be seen with your fiancé. And because if Aurora is going to make a deal with Baresi, he needs to be part of it."

She sensed she was now losing the bit of control she'd had, but she had to be smart with this. "Not if. When. The deal with Baresi will happen, William, because if it doesn't, I'll tell all." She hoped he couldn't see the lie in her eyes. The truth would also hurt her family.

His fingers gripped the arms of the chair until his knuckles turned white. "You wouldn't. You're too…sweet."

Her eyebrows shot up at his choice of words. "Sweet? I was going to enter into a loveless marriage as a business deal. Not sure how sweet that makes me."

"But you didn't go through with it."

It was a fair point. She stood, folding her hands in front of her. "You're protecting your family, and I'm protecting mine. Whatever was between us that night in the garden, and ten minutes ago in this room, can't exist, can it? We both know it. So let's focus on what's important. Our families."

She went to the bed and began folding clothes again, placing them in her suitcase. She certainly hoped that William couldn't tell that her hands were shaking.

Because Gabriella Baresi was terrified. Terrified of what she'd felt only minutes ago, being held in his arms. And terrified that she'd have to make a decision to make good on her threat. In her heart she knew she never would. Never could. Stephen didn't deserve that, and neither did William. Neither did her papa.

She only hoped William didn't call her bluff. Because that would ruin everything.

She'd called him Will. Twice.

Over the last twenty-four hours he'd tried to push that thought aside and failed. Why should it matter so? And yet the sound of her voice, soft and yet strong, speaking the truncated version of his name, repeated over and over. She'd gotten into his head, hadn't she? Into his blood, like a drug he needed more of. The thought sent a shaft of panic through his veins. All those years ago, he'd been looking for thrills, adventure, and the element of danger had been attractive. The reasons why he'd gone off the rails didn't matter. What mattered was that he was worried that reckless person was still inside of him somewhere, waiting to emerge and undo all his hard work.

Was that the real reason he'd insisted he come along? To get his Gabi fix? It couldn't be. No. He was being careful. Protecting his family, like he'd promised to do four years ago. And Gabi was not to blame, not for this. Not for the undeniable attraction and...dammit, need for her. She'd done absolutely nothing to try to tempt or manipulate him. He wasn't sure she was capable of it. No, this was all on him.

Now they were in a rented car, climbing the hill to her family's villa outside Perugia. Umbria was not a region he'd traveled to often, and he was captivated by the rolling hills and abundant olive groves. Gabi drove at eye-watering speeds through the turns, and more than once his fingers tightened in his lap while Gabi seemed perfectly serene.

Perhaps she was. She was getting her way, after all. Except for one sticking point. Stephen would be arriving on Tuesday.

He and his brother had had a huge argument about it. First about the photo, which he'd had to explain as best he could, leaving out the truth that Gabi had so plainly revealed during their argument yesterday. They *did* have chemistry, and a lot of it. She was also right that to ignore it would be a big mistake. Nothing like that scene on the bench—or yesterday's kiss—could happen again.

Once he'd calmed Stephen down, he'd put forward the case for him visiting the Baresi villa. He'd expected it to be a harder sell, but once they'd shifted into business talk Stephen had been far more amenable. It came down to what was good for Aurora, Inc., and the rest be damned.

He loved his brother, but even William was losing patience with Stephen's cold, calculating manner. He'd treated his wedding like a business merger. No wonder Gabi had fled. She deserved better. Even if she'd threatened to reveal the truth to the press, he understood an act of desperation when he saw it. She wasn't mercenary. She was fighting back. He admired that, even if it made her a pain in his neck.

And once more, he was the mess cleaner-upper. Which meant he had to keep her from making good on her threat. He was feeling pulled in about six directions, but he could manage. Finding the right thing to focus on and then coming up with solutions was something he'd discovered he was good at during his time in the trenches at Aurora. It was why his mother had put him in charge of the division, or so she said.

Clean up the mess. Run a division. Make everyone happy. No pressure at all. He'd redeemed himself and proved he was up to the task.

"William?"

"Hmm?" He turned toward her, found her smiling. The sight shouldn't affect him at all, but her full lips curved happily and a light in her eyes sent a warm sensation through his chest. When she was happy, she was breathtaking.

"You weren't listening. Look. You can see the villa from here." She pointed out his window.

A stone villa stood proudly atop the hill. Even at this distance he could tell it wasn't massive but was a good size, tall and strong. Massimo Baresi had built his business and provided for his family. As they wound their way up the drive, he noted healthy-looking olive groves and slopes of leafy grapes. Dust swirled up from their tires as they neared the house, and when they pulled to a stop, a woman who had to be Gabi's mother stepped outside the door, shading her eyes with her hand, a huge smile breaking over her face.

Gabi barely waited for the car to stop before she jumped out and rushed across the gravel, calling, "Mama!"

They hugged tightly for several seconds before Gabi stepped back and turned toward the car.

William took it as his cue, so he opened the door and got out, then shut it carefully behind him.

Signora Baresi said something in Italian as her gaze traveled over him, assessing. William lifted an eyebrow as Gabi laughed, but she gave her head a little shake. He'd ask her later what her mother had said, but there was a twinkle in the older woman's eye so he guessed it couldn't be anything too bad.

"Signora Baresi, it is so good to meet you."

She looked up at him, her eyes sharp. "We were surprised that you were coming with Gabi, and not Stephen."

"He'll join us on Tuesday."

Signora Baresi let her gaze slide to her daughter. "Oh, well, that's good."

Gabi's smile was weak. "It's the first he could get away."

"Get away? You were supposed to be on your honeymoon this week!"

At Gabi's panicked look, William stepped in. "I'm afraid that's my fault," he interjected as smoothly as possible. "I asked Stephen for help on a project. I thought it would keep his mind off things."

Signora Baresi looked at Gabi again. "And you're feeling all right?"

"I'm fine now. Is Giulia here?"

"Tomorrow. She's been staying with friends in Rome since the wedding. I mean, since the wedding was canceled."

Gabi flinched. Clearly the Baresi family had been in favor of the marriage, and the delay wasn't going over well. William quickly realized that Gabi had wanted to come home, but she'd also known that she'd have to keep up the lie of why the wedding didn't happen. She loved her parents. Lying to them had to be killing her.

Did they realize how much she would sacrifice for their well-being?

"It is good to have you home," her mother decreed. "Your father is inside, and I'm making *pollo arrabiata* for dinner."

"Mama. You know that's my favorite."

"Sì, gattina." Her smile was warm as she touched Gabi's face. "I know." Then she looked at William again. "Come. I will show you to your room, Signor Pemberton."

Will tried winning her over with a charming smile. "Please, call me William. Or Will, if you like."

She smiled politely, but William got the idea that he had some work to do where she was concerned. Normally mothers were not his problem. His bank account and the Pemberton charm usually worked fine, but maybe not so much in Italy.

The villa was gorgeous and homey, with oak beams creating an old-country look throughout. Signora Baresi's decorations were warm and welcoming, and Will could understand why Gabi had wanted to come back here. The château was lovely, but this was a home.

Signor Baresi was in the kitchen, fixing a plate of what Will assumed was *antipasti*. A broad smile spread across his face as he saw Gabi enter the room. "Gabriella," he said softly, opening his arms.

"Papa." The way she said it went straight to

William's heart. There was so much affection there, so much love. She went to her father and embraced him, and Will watched as the man closed his eyes and hugged his daughter in return. It made Will miss his own father intensely. Not that they'd ever been the hugging type, but the unconditional welcome? That was familiar, and Will missed it horribly.

"Papa, this is William, Stephen's brother. William is in charge of the fashion division at Aurora."

"Signor Baresi. It's a pleasure to see you again. We met, once a few years ago. And of course, Gabi has told me so much." He held out his hand and Massimo Baresi shook it firmly, not like a man who was about to undergo cancer surgery. But there was something in his color that was off, and he looked tired around the eyes.

"*Benvenuto a* Villa Baresi, William." Massimo glanced at Gabi. "I was sorry to hear that the wedding was postponed, but selfishly I'm hoping that when it is rescheduled I'll be well enough to walk my daughter down the aisle."

"I'm sure she would like nothing more," William replied, smiling at Gabi. "Stephen will be joining us on Tuesday. We want to assure you that nothing will harm your relationship with Aurora. You need to focus on your treatments and recovery."

Massimo wagged his finger at Gabi. "You are

marrying into good people, Gabriella. But then, you have never disappointed us."

Gabi's cheeks pinkened. William wondered why. There was something frightening about being put on a pedestal, wasn't there? Stephen had told him that once. Or maybe Gabi was feeling guilty for lying about her relationship with Stephen. What would her parents think if they knew the truth?

He looked at Gabi closer. For all her "I'll tell the tabloids the truth" talk, he realized that if she did that, she'd also have to come clean with her family. Was she bluffing? He frowned. Maybe. Or maybe she'd risk their disapproval to ensure their business's security. He somehow thought she would. After all, she'd been willing to marry his brother for that very reason, giving up her own life for a few years, and even bearing him a child. She would have been tied to Stephen for life.

He wondered how shaky the Baresi foundation was, really.

"Papa, I'm going to show William to his room. When I come down, I am going to devour that platter with you. I'm starving. William hasn't tried the local prosciutto and salami yet." She kissed his cheek and then looked at him closer. "Are you still allowed to eat it before your surgery?"

"A little, for now. Go. This will be ready soon."

William nodded at Massimo. Signora Baresi went to her husband's side with a smile and wrapped an arm around his waist. The Baresis were a loving and affectionate family, and William liked it. The Pembertons weren't as physically demonstrative, even if love had always been evident and abundant.

"Come on, Will," Gabi said quietly, leading him away. "Your room is up here."

She led him to a guest room on a third floor. An open window let in a warm breeze and there were doors leading to a small balcony. The headboard of the bed was solid wood and sturdy, like the beams of the pitched ceiling. There were flowers on a table, too, and he wondered if they were always there or if they'd been placed especially as a welcome. Overall, it was relaxing and charming. And hot. But he could live with the heat. He was so used to cold and damp in London that he welcomed the Italian summer.

"We don't have air-conditioning. Sorry." Gabi ruffled her hair off her neck. "The villa was built centuries ago, and my grandfather renovated it. We keep at Papa to put in air-con, but so far..."

"It's fine. And quite lovely. Don't worry about me."

"There is a pool. It's especially lovely in the early evening." She smiled softly. "I often swim before bed. I find it cools me off and I sleep better."

His brain instantly conjured up an image of her in a bathing suit, slick with water from the pool, and he knew he would have to avoid an evening swim.

"Thank you." He put down his bag and rolled his shoulders. "Your parents love you very much. It's easy to see. It must be difficult lying to them. I'm sorry about that."

Her face clouded, but before she could answer, there was a knock on the doorframe. "Gabi?"

The disturbed expression gave way to one of joy. "Giulia! You *are* here!"

"Marco and I just got back early from Rome and I came straight here. Are you okay? Truly?" She rattled off something in Italian. William picked up a few familiar words, something about the wedding and Stephen and an apology.

"It is not your fault, not even a little bit. I shouldn't have left you there. I didn't know what else to do. But William has been very helpful." She gave her sister a stern look. "Please don't breathe a word to Papa and Mama, okay? I'm going to fix everything, I promise."

Giulia looked at William and her smile faded. "You were very angry the last time we met."

"I was very panicked the last time we met." He tried a sideways smile, and was gratified when her lips curved a little bit. "Thank you, Giulia, for helping that day, and for your discretion since."

"She is my sister." She said it as if it explained everything, which to William, it did.

"Mama and Papa think there will be a wedding in the future. I don't want them to know any differently. Especially with Papa going for his operation. We can count on you, right?" Gabi pressed forward with the importance of secrecy.

William was surprised Gabi had used the term *we*. But he supposed they were in on it together.

"Of course."

"How is he, really?" Gabi's face fell with worry as she reached for her sister's hand.

William stepped forward. "Why don't you two go and get caught up? I'm fine here. I assume there's internet I can connect to?"

Gabi nodded. "I'll text you the password in a few minutes. And thank you. I'm really quite worried about my father."

He put his hand on her shoulder and squeezed. "Gabi, that's why we're here. You need to be with your family. So go do that. I don't need a nanny or babysitter."

Giulia laughed. "I guess you don't."

For some reason that small joke made William blush, heat traveling to his cheeks. Gabi's cheeks pinkened, too, and they couldn't have that. Giulia couldn't have any idea that there was an attraction between them. Every time they were within two feet of each other, it felt as if sparks lit in his stomach.

"I'll come back and get you for dinner," Gabi said, offering a small smile. "But if there's anything you need, text. I won't be far."

"I'll be fine. Go. Catch up with your family." He leaned over and whispered in her ear. "If you keep your secret, I'll keep my end of the bargain. Remember that."

Her gaze darted up and met his evenly. "How could I forget?"

CHAPTER SIX

"GABI." GIULIA'S VOICE held the kind of significance only a sister knew how to use. "What is going on between you and William Pemberton?"

Gabi fussed with a perfume bottle on her sister's dresser. "Nothing. Don't be ridiculous."

"I'm not." Giulia spun Gabi around with a hand on her arm. "We both know you're not marrying Stephen. So did you leave him because of that very gorgeous man upstairs?"

"No!" She said it too loudly and tempered her voice. "No, of course not." Instead she took a few moments to give Giulia the highlights. "In the end I couldn't do it. Not even for Papa."

Giulia shook her dark curls. "I'm younger than you but even I know that Papa would be furious if he knew you'd made such a bargain."

"You won't tell him, will you?" Gabi lost some of her confidence and looked her sister fully in the face. "I don't think I could bear him being angry at me before his surgery. What if...?"

She let the thought spin out, and knew Giulia felt the same when tears filled her eyes.

"I meant it, Gabi. I won't breathe a word," Giulia promised. She sat down on the bed and patted the mattress beside her. "You are so…good. I feel like a horrible daughter. At least you tried to do something to protect the family. I never came up with such a scheme."

"My idea flopped, so who's the horrible one? Oh, Giulia, how sad is it that I thought it would be better to marry Stephen than have to run the company myself?" Gabi gave a little laugh, but inside guilt was eating her up. Giulia thought she was so good, but before Stephen arrived on the scene she'd been ready to leave everything for a man, with dreams of a wedding and babies in her eyes. She'd been a naive fool. He hadn't been free for either of those things. And it had almost been too late. No, she wasn't the good daughter at all.

"I can't imagine stepping in." Giulia worked in their human resources department. "Don't be too hard on yourself."

"I'm afraid of failing. Of letting Papa down," she confessed.

Giulia reached over and took her hand. "I understand," she said softly. "But you will do fine. You're smart and strong."

She meant the words to be supportive and encouraging, but it added to Gabi's worry that she'd disappoint Giulia, too. She was the older sister, and supposed to set the example.

"How is Marco?" Gabi changed the subject, needing a little levity.

Giulia blushed. "He's fine. Working in the family business. He'll never leave this valley. Which in a way is okay, but in another way…"

"You want to see the world a little?"

She nodded. "Which is silly. We had the most wonderful time in Rome with friends. What's wrong with me?"

"You're both young. What if you spent a year somewhere, working? Like Paris or London?" She wondered if there would be a spot somewhere in Aurora where Gabi could intern. She was a smart girl, and poised. Often underestimated because she was so pretty, but she had a good head on her shoulders.

Of course, asking William—or Stephen—for another favor probably wasn't wise. Still, though, it was something to think about.

"I don't know. Maybe." She shrugged. "I do love him, though. I'm just not ready to settle down."

"You're barely twenty-two. There is lots of time." Gabi squeezed her hand. "At this rate, you'll be married before I will."

She would be stepping up to manage the company, wouldn't she? How much time would she have for relationships and love?

"Not for a while yet," Giulia assured her. "And first we need to look after Papa. And Mama. She is going to find this very difficult. I know I should move out again, but I might be able to help while Papa is sick."

"I'll be staying at my flat in Perugia," Gabi said. "Once the surgery is over and we know where things stand I have to be back to work." She looked into Giulia's eyes. "I screwed up the deal that would help us. So I'm going to do everything I can to make sure Baresi Textiles weathers this storm."

"Maybe William will help you even if Stephen won't." Giulia's gaze was sly. "He couldn't take his eyes off you."

Gabi laughed, even as her cheeks heated. "That's because he's terrified I'll go to the press or do something to hurt Aurora's image."

"Like the photo in the garden?" Giulia's eyes sparkled. "It certainly looked romantic."

"That walk was his idea. And boy, does he regret it." Gabi got up from the bed and rolled her shoulders. "Let's put all of it aside for tonight and enjoy the family being together. Mama's cooking and Papa's jokes and lots of good wine. William needs some Umbrian hospitality." She patted her tummy and laughed. "And after a day or two of Mama's cooking, maybe he will come up with a way to help us."

* * *

An hour later, Gabi went to William's room and knocked. At his easy "come in," she opened the door and found him sitting in a chair, laptop on his knees, typing away on the keys. He smiled at her. "Hi there. Did you catch up with your sister?"

"I did."

"You're close."

"Of course we are." She laughed a little. "We drive each other crazy sometimes, but when it comes down to it, we will always have each other's backs."

"Sounds familiar," he agreed. "Let me send this email and I'll shut down."

She kept her hand on the doorknob. "Papa has food downstairs and you're probably hungry. We could have a little antipasti and I can take you on a tour of the villa, if you like. Dinner will be later."

"Actually, that sounds perfect."

She waited as he typed for a few more seconds, then hit a key with finality and shut the lid on the laptop. "There. I'm all yours."

I wish, she thought, and was glad she hadn't said it out loud. She'd been thinking of him far too often, and long before the kiss happened back in Provence. If he hadn't pushed her away, she might have fallen into bed with him. Giulia's teasing observations had only heightened her awareness. Why couldn't she have met him first, and not Stephen? This story might have had a completely different ending.

The rest of the family was already downstairs. Papa was sitting on a stool nibbling on cold meats and crostini. Giulia was mixing something in a bowl and Mama was checking on her chicken. The smells were unbelievable, and so very much *home*.

"Are you sharing, Papa, or keeping the whole plate to yourself?" He smiled widely and she went forward and kissed his cheek. "Save some for William. And for me. I haven't had good *capicollo* for some time." She reached around him and plucked a piece, popping it into her mouth.

"By all means," he said, sliding the plate over. Gabi selected a few things for herself, but mostly sipped her wine and enjoyed watching William try the different foods as he chatted to her parents. He was so at ease, so perfectly lovely. He laughed at something her father said and his face lit up as he nodded and smiled. She didn't even know what they were talking about. It didn't matter. Her family had made him feel welcome and he'd let them. No airs, no awe. He was just as—or nearly as—rich as Stephen, even without the title. William was…

Perfect. He was perfect. Except that he was Stephen's brother. That was starting to matter to her less and less, and it worried her. At some point she'd let her guard down and started to trust him. Was she wrong to?

Her wine was nearly gone and she'd helped herself to another crostini with truffle pâté when she heard her mother say, "Please, you must call me Lucia. Signora Baresi will not do."

Gabi turned around to find her mother beaming up at William. "All right, Lucia. This was delicious."

"Wait until later. My Lucia makes the best *pollo arrabiata* in Italy." There was a world of pride in her father's voice, and her throat tightened. He had to be okay. He just had to. She looked over at him and realized how exhausted he looked. His skin was pale and there were shadows beneath his eyes. Had the commotion of company tired him out so soon? He tired so easily now. And he'd lost more weight. It wasn't a good sign.

"Maybe William needs a walk to work up his appetite," Gabi suggested, putting down her empty glass. "Would you like me to give you a tour?"

"Very much," he replied, turning his warm gaze from her mother to her. It made her a little weak in the knees, and the warm glow from the glass of wine wasn't helping.

It was a little easier to establish some distance between them once they were outside. First she took him along the patio and pool, and then the gardens.

"Your father was getting tired," William observed, his voice somber. "You suggested the walk to give him time to rest, didn't you?"

She nodded. "I'll be glad when the surgery happens and we can get on with his treatment. I can't help thinking that every day we wait erodes his chances at recovery."

"A few more days, that's all," William reassured her. He reached for her hand. "Stay positive. He'll need that."

"I know you're right. And I don't mean to bring down the mood. I'm supposed to be giving you a tour." She smiled and removed her hand from his clasp, which had felt far too good. "These are Mama's vegetable gardens. She used to tend them by herself, but now she has a local boy come in two days a week to look after the grass and weeds." Most of the vegetables that graced their table came from their own gardens. It was a point of pride with Lucia.

"If that snack was anything to go by, your mother is a marvelous cook," William said as they ambled along, graciously accepting the subject change. "And you've inherited her talents, haven't you? The meal you made at the château was delicious."

Gabi thought for a moment. "We're not poor and we've never been poor. This is a lovely vill and my parents have renovated it through the years as the business grew and things got easier. But we haven't had staff or servants, either. Mama taught both of us how to cook and how to clean. By the time I was twelve I was doing all my own laundry. I've been helping in the kitchen since I was old enough to stand on a little stool to see the counter. I'm glad of it. I have my own flat in Perugia, and I enjoy keeping it and cooking for myself. Even if cooking for one can be a bit lonely."

Particularly since her relationship ended. At least once a week Luca had come over for dinner and…

Gabi didn't like to think of it now. She'd been so foolish and trusting.

"Surely you haven't been too lonely," William ventured, chuckling. "You're a beautiful woman, Gabi. And accomplished."

"Since you're prying, I'll tell you that I was seeing someone for quite a while. It didn't work out."

"I'm sorry."

"Not as sorry as I am." The words were bitter and sharp.

He halted and faced her. "What happened?"

Gabi lifted an eyebrow. "Well, if I'm honest, I was a fool. I wanted forever. A wedding and babies and a family. I really thought that was where we were heading. But he already had those things…with his wife."

She'd shocked him. His lips dropped open and his eyes widened with surprise. "Oh. From how you said that, I'm assuming you didn't know."

"No. But I should have, looking back. There were red flags I ignored. So I got my heart crushed and felt incredibly stupid all at the same time. Life lessons, you know?"

"When did this happen?"

"Last winter."

It didn't take a rocket scientist to figure out that this had happened only a few months before her engagement to Stephen. "I see," he said quietly, and started walking again.

She caught up with him within a few steps and sighed. "Yes, I can see you do. I was bitter and jaded and Stephen and I had been friendly for a while by then. So fool me twice. Instead of being smart and using my head, I let my emotions carry me into another bad situation."

"But for honorable reasons," William added.

They were at the olive groves now, and out of view of the villa. "Perhaps. Or perhaps that was my excuse. Stephen was offering me what I thought I was going to have—a big wedding and a baby and security. And I was so angry and disillusioned that for a while I figured love didn't matter. It got in the way. It…hurt."

"But it does matter."

She shrugged. "To me it does, and it took me getting an hour from the altar to realize it. Either way, I have to have my eyes open now. No more foolish decisions."

William sighed and put his hands in his pockets. They had paused at the top of a hill, and the olive trees sloped down and away from them, running into a long, green valley. "It's beautiful here."

"Isn't it? I understand Mama and Papa never wanting to leave, although they've been talking about moving closer to the city, into something smaller, for a while now. Even more so since Papa became ill. The ironic thing? They had a house in Perugia and they sold it when the economy shifted. The villa was more important to them." She knew her voice sounded sad, but she couldn't help it. She loved the villa and the rolling hills surrounding it. "But it's a large house with large grounds and a lot of upkeep."

"And they either need help with it, or need to change their situation."

She nodded. "And I'm not sure they want to hire help. It's not just the cost. I think it would seem less…theirs somehow. I don't know if that makes sense."

"Not really. I was born with the proverbial silver spoon. But just because I'm different doesn't make their perspective any less valid. It's a shame. I can tell you love it here."

"It's home," she said simply. It was the place she came back to even as she loved her life and flat in the city. There were so many memories here. And so much love.

William held out his hand. "Let's keep walking. We can circle around the grounds and make room for dinner."

She hesitated, then put her hand in his. It fit so perfectly, her fingers clasped in his slightly larger, stronger ones. That curl of awareness was back, and she was once again unsure what to do about it. The situation was far too complicated to make it more so by getting involved romantically. But nothing bad would come from holding hands, would it? She thought back to her time spent with Stephen. Holding hands had never been his thing.

"You're different from your brother," she said.

"How so?"

She shrugged. "I don't know how to say this without seeming uncomplimentary. He's very polite and charming, but also a bit…"

"Cold?"

"Reserved," she amended.

"He's always been a little more somber than the rest of us. I think it's a first-child thing, really. And something about the burden and weight of expectation. He's the first son, heir to a title and estate. He feels responsible not only for our mother and the legacy he's left with, but us, too.

Honestly, it's a burden he places mostly on him-self. But you know the old saying, right? Heavy lies the head that wears the crown?"

She did know it, and nodded. "We are…were, anyway, friends. I like him very much. But he's not really easygoing."

"No. I'm trying very hard to understand his motives in all this. I guess his whole world was upside down and there was nothing he could do to make it right. The one thing he thought he could fix was Mother. He was determined to see her through her grief."

"And I was part of his plan."

"Stephen is a great one for making plans. Usu-ally they're good ones. This one was not. But only, I think, because it came from the wrong place. A broken place."

"You're very understanding. And…thoughtful. Not many men I know would understand those feelings so well."

He squeezed her fingers. "I have a big soft spot for my brother. I see his flaws but I know the heart underneath. He would do anything for his family." He looked away over the valley and Gabi saw his throat bob as he swallowed. "He saved me, you know. Gave me tough love and support and a shoulder to cry on, too."

"He did?"

"Four years ago. Seems like a lifetime away now. I was twenty-four, done school, wasting my life, partying all the time. I had no direction, so I drifted in the wrong one. Hung around with the wrong people and did wrong things." He paused. "I think deep down I'd always resented him being the center of everything and me being...less important. I started thinking of him as Saint Stephen, and I was determined to be what he wasn't. I wasn't the heir. I could do what I wanted."

"You thought no one cared what you did."

He didn't look at her, but she took his silence for agreement. He was quiet for so long Gabi thought that was going to be the end of the story.

Finally he sniffed and rolled his shoulders. "He found me one day, in my London flat, still high on drugs and booze. I'd promised him I'd stop and it had lasted two whole days before I scored again. Stephen came in, put me in the shower, cleaned up my flat and took me to rehab. He was with me every step of the way. And so was my father. When I was clean, my father offered me a job at Aurora. Put his faith in me even though I didn't deserve it. There was only one way I could repay both of them. I had to live up to their faith in me because I loved them, too."

Tears had sprung into Gabi's eyes as William told the story. "Addiction is a terrible thing."

"Getting clean has been the hardest and best thing I've ever done. I told you before that I can't repay my father. That's true. He's gone now." His voice was thick with emotion, and Gabi realized he was still grieving, too. "But it's also the reason why I have been so determined to make this right for Stephen. He saved my life. Saved me from myself. I owe him everything."

She paused, tugging on his hand. "So this thing between you and me, this 'back and forth, ignore it most of the time and acknowledge it occasionally' attraction, it's eating at you because of your loyalty to Stephen."

"Exactly."

"And it eats at me because of my father, and the company. Because that's where my allegiance lies."

"It's damned inconvenient, isn't it?"

But he wasn't scowling this time, not like he'd been in France.

"I really am sorry about that photo on the bench."

"I wasn't really angry at you, Gabi. I was angry at myself."

"I know."

The soft admission swirled around them. It had been barely over a week and already she felt she knew him better than she'd ever known his brother. She looked up into his eyes and melted a little. "This is going to sound awful and complicated and a million other things, but I really wish I could kiss you again, Will."

He drifted closer, his head blocking the sun

from blazing onto her face. Instead it created a halo around his hair. She wanted to run her fingers into it, pull his face down to hers. But she wouldn't. She'd issued the invitation. She'd let him decide if he wanted to take her up on it.

"You shouldn't say things like that."

"It's very inadvisable. And I just finished telling myself I was done with wrong decisions." Her voice was barely a whisper. Somewhere in the olive groves birds sang, and she faintly registered their lilting song, but her sense of touch was overriding everything, making her attuned to his every move and breath.

"And I'd be a wrong decision."

"After what you just told me? Don't you think so?"

"A kiss," he said, his voice uncertain. "That's all we're talking about here."

"There are no photographers," she whispered. "No one will know."

"I'll know," he answered, even closer now, so close she was dying to close the gap and press herself against his strong chest.

"Then it'll be our little secret."

"Damn you."

His hand curled around her neck, but not in anger and frustration as it had the last time. This time it was a caress, a strong, yet tender touch as his fingers slid beneath her hair to press against the muscles of her neck. Before she could think, she tilted her head into his touch, her eyes drifting closed as the sun washed over her face. The light was gone again as he followed her movements, touching his lips to hers.

At the moment of contact, her mouth followed his lead, like a sunflower arching to the morning sun. *Girasole*, she thought, opening her mouth wider beneath his, letting the kiss blossom and grow. She was the flower, he was the sun, and she couldn't get enough of his light and warmth.

"Gabi," he whispered, then trailed his lips from her mouth to her jaw, and then back to the sensitive spot just below her earlobe. "You taste so good, Gabi."

Every single nerve ending in her body was alive. "Mmm," she answered, stretching into the contact. "You feel good. You're warm and hard and..." She couldn't finish the thought. His mouth skittered over the tender skin of her neck and she gasped. "Will," she murmured, turning fully into his arms, and they kissed again, a little wilder now.

He walked her backward until she stumbled a little, and then he did the most amazing and surprising thing. He lifted her against him so that her feet dangled inches off the ground, and carried her to the shade of an olive tree. The bark was warm and hard beneath her back, providing a bolster as Will pressed close again. Not close enough. Never enough. But enough for now. It had to be.

He kissed her for long minutes, until it seemed their control hung by a mere thread. He'd unbuttoned the top of her dress and kissed his way to her cleavage, though he'd stopped at her lace bra, much to her relief and disappointment. Her hair was a mess from rubbing against the tree trunk, and she was sure she had whisker burn down her jaw and neck. The simple cotton skirt she wore had stayed in place, but the thin material had done little to hide his desire.

And Gabi had explored, too. Her fingers had skimmed up his ribs and then pulled his shirt out of his jeans so she could explore the warm, hard body beneath. She'd splayed her hands over his back and shoulder blades, pulling him close, wanting things she had no right to want. She was on fire and didn't care. Nothing could have prepared her for this. Everything was different from anything she'd ever known. Chemistry, sure. But more than that. There was a connection between them that went deeper than attraction.

"We need to stop," he murmured, stilling his hands on her arms. "Gabi, we need to stop now."

"I know." Her breath caught as she tried to slow it. "Will, this is so complicated...what I said back in Provence..."

His golden gaze clung to hers. "You needed to come home. I understand. And you played your cards to get here. I respect that, too, even though it meant I didn't get my own way."

"It's going to be okay, though, right?"

He lifted his hand and brushed a finger over her cheek. "I want to say yes, but this is too…" He growled. "It's such a damned mess. If only it had been anyone but you."

"If only I'd met you first…"

He reached down and gripped her fingers tightly. "Don't say that. We have to focus on doing the right thing here."

Her heart hammered as her chest rose and fell with breathlessness. She knew what he meant— minimizing the fallout from the wedding, and to secure Baresi Textiles to the benefit of both companies. He was right, but that didn't address the very real problem of them. "And what about us?"

He looked away and his jaw tightened. "Gabi, I don't see how there can be an us. It would be better if we could be friends. And business associates." He swallowed tightly and his gaze touched hers again. "We leave sex out of it."

Sex. For a flash of a moment that word pulsed through her, leaving an indelible impression of what that glorious event might be like. Sex with Will. Desire flooded her body but she tamped it down ruthlessly.

She stepped away from the trunk of the olive tree and heaved a sigh that was full of frustration and resignation. "Even if I know you're right, I don't have to like it." Gabi kicked at a small rock with her toe. "I have such a talent for meeting men at the exact time they're unavailable."

William chuckled a bit, relieving some of the tension around them. "Everyone has a skill," he said, and she couldn't help but laugh despite herself.

"I'd like to develop a different one." She lifted her chin. "So what, we go back to the villa and that's it, friends only?"

"I think we have to. For everyone's sake, including ours. It's messy, but I also don't want to hurt you, and I think I could."

She wondered if she could hurt him. She doubted it. And that alone was reason enough to walk away. Her eyes burned with regret and sadness. "We should get back, then."

"Can I kiss you once more?" His eyes pleaded with her. "I don't want the last time to be, well, the last time. One more to take away with me."

Torture. This was torture of the sweetest kind.

She lifted her face and opened her lips slightly. "One more."

He cradled her face in his hands and kissed her with such gentleness she wasn't sure what to do with all the feelings that crowded her heart. Why did it have to be this way? Why did the perfect guy have to show up now and be completely unavailable? Why did he have to be so damned ethical and loyal?

He pulled away, leaving her empty and bereft. Without speaking, and now without holding hands, they made their way back toward the villa, where her parents and sister waited. The day after tomorrow Stephen would arrive. The day after that her father would have his surgery. And then the Pemberton brothers would walk out of her life forever.

CHAPTER SEVEN

WILLIAM COULDN'T REMEMBER the last time he'd had such a wonderful meal.

It wasn't just the food, though that was spectacular. The chicken was to die for, and he sopped up the sauce with the most amazing bread. Then there was almond cake for dessert, and the most delicious wine to go with it all. But the real wonderfulness was in spending time with the Baresi family.

Giulia's boyfriend, Marco, was there, so the table rounded out at six. It was clear he'd been close to the family for a while, and Will grinned at how he teased Lucia and made her laugh and how he'd wink at Giulia and make her blush. Despite his illness, Massimo's laugh was big and booming, and Will could tell they were a family who enjoyed being together.

The Pembertons were like that as well, but it had been different since his father's death. Not so much laughter. An empty spot at the table when they were all together. Cedric had died and taken a lot of the family joy with him. Will had missed it, he realized. And if anything happened to Massimo, the Baresi family wouldn't be the same, either.

He pushed away his plate and looked across the table at Gabi. She was smiling and watching her family, too, and her gaze slid to William's and held. She was thinking the same thing, wasn't she? She loved them so much. Perhaps her agreement with his brother had been impulsive, but he still believed she'd done it for her family. She'd do anything for them.

Massimo laughed and her gaze was diverted for a moment, but when she looked back again, he saw the certainty in her eyes. Even without help from Aurora, Inc., Gabi would do whatever she could to keep the business going. She had that kind of burning passion inside her, didn't she? He should know. He'd had to turn it away earlier in order to do the right thing.

Stephen was an idiot.

When dinner was over, he pulled Gabi aside. "Tomorrow, I think we should meet to discuss Baresi's current situation and go over the notes I made. When Stephen arrives, I want to present him with a plan he can't say no to. One that will keep Baresi profitable and stable, enable your father to take the time off to have the treatment he needs, and that also benefits Aurora."

"One that keeps the majority of ownership in our hands?" she asked.

"That's never been a question. Of course. I want Aurora to invest in it. And I want you to be able to use our resources so you're not trying to do this alone, Gabi, but you would still have control."

"All right. Tomorrow morning, after breakfast."

He nodded.

"We should join the others." The family had taken drinks out to the patio, where the breeze was refreshing, and Gabi turned on her heel and walked away. William followed her outside and took a seat with everyone else. But his earlier joy had dissipated. Gabi had followed his guidance impeccably—friends, business, but no intimacy at all. It was what he wanted, and what had to happen.

But it left him distinctly unsatisfied, because his heart didn't always follow logic a hundred percent. After this afternoon, his heart wanted more. He was dangerously close to falling for her, and he wasn't entirely sure it wasn't because she was supposed to be off-limits. Worse, he knew she could be a huge distraction, when he'd carefully built a new life and wanted to keep on the right course. All in all, Gabriella Baresi did not fit into his life.

So he stared into his cup and frowned, and after a few minutes, excused himself to go back up to his room.

Gabi wasn't sure what to expect when she saw Stephen again, and her chest was cramped as anxiety took hold on Tuesday morning. He was scheduled to arrive around eleven. The last time she'd seen him, the last time they'd spoken, was the night before the non-wedding.

Will had been the buffer all this time. She hadn't even had to speak to Stephen on the phone. And today Will had offered to be there for her first meeting with his brother. But Gabi said no. She had to face Stephen on her own, if she were to have any self-respect and any agency with him at all.

Besides, she and Stephen had been friends. Their friendship demanded she be honest and up front with him, and not hide behind his brother. It wasn't fair to put Will in the middle any more than he already was.

Ever punctual, Gabi saw the cloud of dust announcing Stephen's arrival at precisely seven minutes to eleven. Her stomach was in knots. Will had agreed to remain upstairs until Gabi had a chance to talk to Stephen, and Giulia had gone to work. That left her parents, and the awkward realization that they still thought that Gabi and

Stephen were going to set a new date. Things had been easy between her and Stephen before. She hoped they wouldn't be overtly awkward now.

Oh, *mea culpa*.

Stephen parked his rental and she stepped to the doorway, feeling as if she might throw up. What a stir she'd caused. And now he'd come all the way out here. There was no way he was happy about it.

When he stepped out of the car she remembered how different he was from Will. Only slightly taller, but with darker hair, darker eyes and a squarer jaw. When he smiled he epitomized tall, dark and handsome. But right now he wasn't smiling. He wasn't really showing any emotion at all as he looked at her. Then he shut the door and stepped around the hood to approach the house, and his mouth softened the smallest bit.

"Gabriella."

"Hello, Stephen." Always Stephen. Never Steve. Or any other endearment. That just occurred to her now, and yet in a short amount of time she'd found herself shortening William to Will…in her head, and sometimes that's what came out of her mouth, too.

He leaned in and they bussed cheeks. "Do your parents know?" he murmured, before pulling away.

She met his gaze, her stomach quaking. "No," she whispered.

His dark eyes cooled. "So they think we're still engaged."

Gabi swallowed against a growing lump in her throat. "Y-yes. Are you able to…you know… pull that off?"

He smiled then, warm and lovely. "My dear Gabriella, I've spent a lifetime smiling at people I don't know or don't like. It won't be a problem. The bigger question is, will you be able to act like a convincing fiancée?"

She wanted to weep. His words were delivered with a smile but were so sharp and cutting. "Stephen, we were friends, remember? I'd like us to stay friends."

"You left me at the altar," he said quietly. "I deserved better."

She held her tongue because, first of all, he was right. And secondly, she desperately wanted to call him out on insisting on the marriage in the first place, but right now she needed him on her side. Tonight her father would be admitted into the hospital. Later tomorrow he'd have surgery. The question of the company needed to be settled.

"Let's not talk out here. Come inside to the library where we can have some privacy."

They entered the house and right away her mother was there, greeting Stephen, offering refreshment. He switched on the charm and accepted a drink of something cold; Massimo came forward to shake his hand and the two spoke warmly. It couldn't all be an act, could it? Stephen was angry with her but he'd always been so great to her parents. When Massimo mentioned how good it was for him to be here for Gabi while he had his operation, Gabi wanted to choke. She didn't want solace from Stephen, not anymore. But she'd love to have William beside her, she realized. How things had changed in such a short time.

After pleasantries, Gabi led him into the small library, which was really a home office with several bookshelves. She shut the door and let out a breath. "Thank you."

"I have no problem with your parents, Gabi. They're innocent in all this."

"But I'm not."

"No, you're not." He put his glass down on a table and turned to face her. "If you were going to bolt, why the hell did you say yes in the first place?"

It was hard to breathe, but she had to own up to everything. "Because I wanted security for my family. Because we were friends and I trusted you. And because I'd had my heart broken and my dreams shattered and I thought I could have what I wanted without the messiness of being in love."

His mouth dropped open. "What?"

It was the thing she'd confessed to William,

but hadn't to her own fiancé. "I loved someone, Stephen. I thought I was pregnant and while the timing wasn't great, I was happy. I want a partner and babies. When I told him about it, he was so angry. You see, he was already married. Thank God the test was negative."

Stephen ran his hand through his hair and shook his head. "Why didn't you tell me this?"

"I was afraid. And at the time I was really focusing on Baresi and doing what I had to in order for us to weather my father's illness."

When he said nothing, she spoke again. "Our motivations were the same, weren't they? You'd had your heart broken, too. You wanted to put your mother's mind at ease. Give her something positive after your father's death. I don't blame you for that."

His gaze sharpened. "But you do blame me for something, don't you?"

Heat rushed to her face. "What good does blame do? You have every right to be angry with me. In the end I couldn't go through with it, and I ran. I panicked. I caused a great deal of…inconvenience. And I'm sorry for that. I truly am."

"You're sorry."

"Yes! And wanted to tell you that in person."

Stephen was quiet for several moments. He picked up his glass and drank again, then wandered around the room, glancing at shelves, making Gabi more nervous by the second. What was he thinking? Why wasn't he saying anything?

When she was ready to burst, he turned back to her. "But that's not why I'm here, is it? For apologies?"

She bit down on her lip, considering her response. "I know you were hurt before, and I'm sorry that I added to it by my actions."

His nostrils flared, the only outward sign that her words had hit some sort of sore spot. "Don't worry, Gabriella. We both know this wasn't going to be a real marriage, with love and hearts and flowers. You didn't hurt me."

Maybe not. But she'd caused him great embarrassment, and she sensed that was almost as bad. Maybe worse. Feelings you could hide away from the world. Public humiliation was out there for all to see. And, in his case, comment on incessantly.

He stepped closer. "So I'll ask you again, Gabi. Why am I really here? It's not to make amends. I know that. Particularly since it wasn't you who invited me. It was Will."

Her annoyance came bubbling up and she spoke before she could think better of it. "Would you have taken my call?"

"Probably not. Will seems to think that Aurora should still invest in Baresi. I disagree."

Cold ran down her body. She hadn't thought this would be an easy meeting, but she hadn't expected a downright refusal. "Please," she whis-

pered, "don't punish my father because of what
I did."

"I like your father. But this is business, *cara*."

The way he said the endearment made her
want to slap his face. "This is not business. This
is taking it out on me. Punishing me."

He shrugged and her temper flared again. "A
shrug? That's your answer? Doing business with
Baresi is good for Aurora and you know it! Making a deal wouldn't have been any sacrifice on
your part, just the opposite. But you tacked on the
condition of marriage as a way of 'helping each
other.' That isn't business. That's personal. And
you're making it personal again now."

He was silent again. How could he do that?
How could he stay so calm and implacable?

"Well," he finally said, drawing out the word
for emphasis, "I'm the head of acquisitions. So it
doesn't matter if it's personal or not. I still have to
sign off on it. Our contract with Baresi remains
the same, don't worry. I'm not canceling it. I'm
just not furthering our investments."

For a moment, it felt to Gabi as if her heart
stopped. Baresi was struggling; not in danger
of closing its doors—yet—but the last few years
had been difficult. No one knew the business
better than her father. But his surgery, recovery
and then rounds of chemotherapy meant he'd be
out of the office for months. They couldn't afford
a further decline. And Gabi would do her level

best, but if anything happened to Baresi Textiles, how would her parents live? Papa wasn't old, but he wasn't a young man, either. He and Mama needed to be thinking about working less and enjoying each other more.

The cold knot settled in her gut. "So that's it, then," she said, taking a step back. "I've ruined everything." She was angrier than she could ever remember being in her life. "Because I couldn't go through with a sham marriage. I thought we were friends. I see how wrong I was."

She turned to walk away, and had almost reached the door when he called out, "What are you going to tell your parents?"

"I don't know. I'm not going to cause Papa any more worry today, not when he has surgery tomorrow. But don't worry, Stephen, I'll figure it out. I'll figure it all out."

She swept out of the room, biting her lip so hard she thought it might bleed. Then she went straight for the stairs. She couldn't talk to her parents like this. She had to get herself together. And William needed to speak to Stephen, too.

Will's door was shut and she knocked quietly. There were footsteps, then he opened the door and his face blanked with shock. "What the hell did he say? You look ready to commit murder."

"I need to calm down and I don't want to rant at you because he's your brother and you love him. So please, go speak to him about whatever you need to and leave me here to calm down."

"You asked him about the deal and he said no, didn't he?"

"He said a lot more, too. He's very angry at me, Will. And I'm very angry at me. I put myself in this position and now my family is being punished for it. Please, let me lick my wounds in private."

He nodded, but as he moved past her in the doorway, he squeezed her hand. "Wait here. I'll come back and we'll talk."

"All right."

He left and she shut the door quietly, then went to the chair he'd been sitting in and sank into it. He'd left his phone, and his laptop was on a small table, still open. He really did trust her, she realized. While she hadn't always liked Will's decisions or attitude, she could say this for him: he'd always been honest with her. Always.

He'd always displayed impeccable integrity and loyalty. But then, so had Stephen, or so she thought. Was she being foolish, trusting Will?

She leaned her head back against the chair and sniffled. She didn't know what to say to her father. He'd been so happy when she'd announced her engagement. "I know he'll make sure everything is all right," Massimo had said. "He'll look after you." And in looking after her, Massimo had known that Stephen would ensure nothing would happen to Baresi. That was all gone now.

Her father had trusted him, too, because she'd let him. Maybe it was time to stop being angry at Stephen and take responsibility for her part in it. And that meant coming clean with her parents.

The timing sucked. But if anything happened to her father tomorrow, she didn't want their last words to be based on a lie.

CHAPTER EIGHT

WILL STARED AT his brother. "So your answer is no. Even though I've given you the numbers that prove this could be profitable for us, and not an act of charity. And by the way, even if it were an act of charity, it would be the right thing. Aurora has done business with Barcsi for over two decades."

"My answer is no."

"Because of your pride."

Stephen stared at William for a long moment. "Why do you care so much?"

Will struggled to keep his face schooled. What he felt for Gabi wasn't any of his brother's business, especially since it wasn't going to go anywhere. "Because she's a nice woman who got caught up in a lot of stuff. Because she did the right thing in the wrong way, and now you're making a point of punishing her entire family for it."

Stephen's expression darkened. "What do you mean?"

Will met his brother's eyes and unease slid through his gut. In four years, he'd never really been at odds with Stephen. To be so now hurt, and he still very much felt like the younger, less wise brother. And yet he knew, deep down, that Stephen was wrong.

"You know I love you. But I can't pretend that this whole arrangement was okay. I told you that at the beginning. I admire her for not going through with it. It shows an integrity that you didn't, Stephen. And yes, she could have done it differently and caused less fuss. But you're punishing her for doing the right thing."

"Oh, my God. You love her." Stephen cursed and wiped a hand over his face. "Ten days. Has it even been ten days? And she's wrapped you around her little finger."

Will tamped down his anger. "My loyalty is with you, Stephen. It always will be. It doesn't mean I always have to agree with you. You told me when I screwed up. Well, you screwed up this time. Do the right thing here. Buy an interest in Baresi. It's right for Aurora."

"I'm heading back to Rome, and then home. And, William? Don't issue an order for me again."

Will's heart lurched, hating that their relationship was suffering, and yet certain in his gut that his motives were in the right place. "If that's the way you want it."

"It is."

"Fine. I'll handle everything here."

Stephen laughed bitterly. "There's nothing to handle."

Will went to the library door and held it open for his brother. His disappointment was profound. It was so unlike Stephen to be petty and mean. William had to believe that it was pain and pride wrapped up into one.

"If you think that," Will said quietly, "I'm disappointed in you." And just like that, their roles were reversed.

Stephen stopped at the door and met Will's gaze. "Don't lecture me, little brother."

Then he left—straight down the hallway and out the front door, without saying goodbye to anyone. Why had he even come?

William wasn't just mad. He was horribly, horribly disappointed in his brother.

Lucia came to the library door. "William? Has Stephen left? Did Gabi go with him?"

"No, Mama." Gabi's steady voice sounded behind her mother, and Will looked over Lucia's shoulder to catch Gabi's gaze. Her chin was set with a determined tilt and there was no biting down on her lip. Her eyes were dry. When she'd gone to his room, he'd thought her on the verge of tears. The woman in front of him was anything but.

"I don't understand." Lucia looked from Gabi to William and then back again.

"You will." She went forward and hugged Lucia tightly. "I need to talk to you and Papa. In the kitchen, okay?"

"All right," Lucia said, but her eyes were worried as she moved off to find Massimo.

Will looked down at Gabi. "Are you sure you want to do this?"

She nodded. "It's time I told the truth. There should be no lies between Papa and me tomorrow." Her gaze locked with his. "You do not have to be there for it, but I would appreciate the support if you want to give it. I understand if not. Stephen is your brother, and I know where your loyalties lie."

Will clenched his teeth. "I won't go behind my brother's back and go against his wishes. That's true. But I can certainly stand beside a friend when they do a difficult thing."

"You're a very decent human being," she murmured.

"I try to be. Stephen taught me that. That he's somehow forgotten hurts me. But I'll sit with you today. And tomorrow, too, if you want me to. I know it's going to be a long, rough day."

He didn't want to have to choose. In fact, he refused to. Being there for a friend during a difficult time should not be a crisis of loyalty. And if it was, he and Stephen were going to have even bigger words once Will was back in Paris.

Gabi sat at the table, with William beside her and her mother across from them. Massimo shuffled into the room and settled himself in a chair with a sigh, his jovial face tight with concern. Gabi met her father's gaze and said, "I'm sorry, Papa. It's time I told you and Mama the truth."

"It has to do with Stephen?"

"Yes, and me, and a foolish mistake that I'm going to make right. I haven't been honest with you, and I don't want there to be lies between us."

Their gazes held a long time, full of unsaid words. She knew he understood when he answered softly, "Me, either, *gattina*." Oh, how it hurt for them both to consider his mortality like this. He couldn't die. He just couldn't.

Will sat beside her and put his hand over hers for a brief moment. She was so glad he was here.

"Mama, Papa…" She looked at both of them and felt her heart in her throat. "I wasn't sick the day of the wedding. I ran away because I couldn't go through with it. The Pembertons made up my illness so there wouldn't be a scandal. Or as much of one, anyway."

Gabi had expected the shocked looks on their faces, so she carried on, since that was just the opening and not anywhere near the worst part.

"The truth is, our engagement wasn't what it seemed. It was more of an...agreement."

Massimo and Lucia looked at each other, then back at Gabi. "You mean you were not in love with him," Lucia said, her voice low.

"No, Mama, I wasn't. And I'm not. We were friends. Or at least I thought we were. Now I'm not so sure." Her nose burned a little, but she wouldn't cry. She'd screwed up but Stephen had disappointed her, too. Maybe she was a horrible judge of character.

But then she looked over at Will and saw the reassurance in his eyes, and her confidence returned.

"But why?" Massimo asked. "Why would you agree to marry him if you didn't love him? Your mama and me...oh, Gabriella. You were raised in a house where there was always love. Why would you settle for less?"

"I know, Papa, I know!" The words came out in a flood. "In the end, that was why I couldn't do it. I couldn't marry someone I didn't love, even if it meant having all the security in the world."

Massimo's face changed. "Security?"

"Papa." She reached across the table and took his hand. It was still so strong and warm, as it had always been. "I agreed to something I shouldn't have, and I'm sorry. Please listen before you get angry."

"I don't like the sound of this, Gabriella."

She sighed. "I know." Will's hand rested on her shoulder, giving her courage. She sent him a look of gratitude and then faced her father again.

"You know as well as I do that Baresi has been struggling. Not desperately, but the market has been tough and we've felt the pinch. I'm an accountant, Papa. I know how to read the sheets. Then, with your diagnosis, and the long treatment ahead of you…all I could see was a ship without a captain, no one to take the wheel. I started to fear for our financial situation, so when Stephen and I became friends, I might have told him a little of what we were facing. He was the one who came up with the plan, Papa, but he's not to blame. I considered it and agreed to it, which makes me just as guilty."

"What plan?"

The question was delivered with a sharpness that stole her breath. Still, she deserved her father's anger and disappointment and so told them everything.

Silence fell around the table when she was done. Lucia's mouth had dropped open and Massimo's brows were pulled together so tightly they nearly met above his nose.

She couldn't stand the silence so she carried on. "Papa… Baresi is everything. I wanted to do this so the legacy wouldn't be threatened. But it was the wrong thing, and I couldn't do it."

"Thank God for that," Lucia murmured.

"Did you not trust me to make sure the company was in good hands?" Massimo asked, and it killed Gabi to hear the hurt in his voice.

"Of course I trust you! Papa, you have never let me down. I was just so scared. When the doctor said it was cancer, all I wanted to do was look after this for you. To make sure Baresi flourished so it would be waiting for you when you were better." Her eyes burned. "I was so afraid of messing up and not being up to this challenge. You put your faith in me to step in but I'm not sure I can do this."

Will's hand still rested on her shoulder and she reached up and clasped it briefly. "I'm sorry, Papa. I lost my head for a while and made some stupid decisions. But I've got it back on right now. Tomorrow you're going to have your operation and I'm going to make sure the company thrives, even without Aurora's backing. It's time for me to step up and I'll do everything in my power to make sure I don't let you down."

"*Gattina*, why did you not talk to me? To your mother? We would have worked through this together."

Lucia leaned forward. "You didn't have to take this all on yourself. We're a family."

"I thought you had enough to worry about. I didn't want to be a burden." She sniffed now, as relief at unloading the secret started to creep in. "Papa, I wasn't going to tell you the truth because

I didn't want to upset you before your operation. But today I realized…it isn't right to have lies between us. I failed but I won't again, I promise."

Massimo's eyes softened. He got up from his chair and came around the table, and Gabi rose and went into his arms. His safe, warm, strong arms that had always been there for her since the day she was born. A bit weaker now, certainly, and she tried not to let the fear take over.

"Gabriella Angelica Baresi, you have not failed anyone. I believe in you. I should have told you this before, but I didn't want to add any pressure when you were planning a wedding." He laughed a little, and stepped back so he could look into her eyes. "You know I made all the necessary arrangements at the office for the month I am recovering. I also had papers drawn up. If anything does happen to me, Gabi, the company is yours. You might be a numbers woman, but you're smart and resourceful and you love what I've built. I trust you to look after your mother and sister. And I didn't tell you because I felt it would be a huge burden on your shoulders while you were on your way to marry Stephen."

"You said you were glad I'd be taken care of."

"It put my mind at ease. I knew if anything happened and you took over Baresi, Stephen would be able to look after *you*. I was never expecting him to look after my company. You might not have faith in yourself, but I have faith in you. And you could not let me down. Ever."

She put her shoulders back. "I can look after myself."

"She sure can." Will finally spoke.

Massimo looked over Gabi's shoulder. "And what's your part in all this? You're Stephen's brother. You said you were here to check on local business interests and to escort Gabi home until Stephen could join her. Clearly that's not true, either."

Will shook his head, but Gabi admired his calm. "No, it's not. Well, some of it's true. I did escort Gabi home, at my insistence, not hers. And I have been checking up on local interests. Baresi is one of them. Initially I took on the role of damage control after the wedding didn't happen. Giulia helped me find Gabi, and then we went to the family château in France to wait out the media storm. Over that time I've come to see how stupid my brother has been, both in suggesting such an arrangement and—"

It was if he'd suddenly realized he'd said something wrong. Will pursed his lips and frowned.

"And?" Lucia prodded him.

"And I like your daughter," he said, almost as if daring them to defy him. "She's a good person who wanted nothing more than to take care of her family, and she was willing to do it at her own personal cost. While the idea was flawed, her loyalty and love were not. I presented my brother with a proposal to partner with Baresi, something that would benefit both you and Aurora. He turned it down, because of his pride. But if there is anything I can do to be of help, I will. I won't go against my family, but as I told Gabi before this conversation, I'm definitely willing to help a friend."

His gaze went to Gabi's. "And despite the unorthodox circumstances, I do believe we've become friends."

She nodded, overwhelmed by his speech. "Yes, we have. Thank you, Will."

"You're welcome."

Will looked up at Massimo. "*Signore*, if there is anything at all you need, I hope you will ask. My brother is head of acquisitions, but I'm the head of my division, and I'll do what I can to ensure Aurora's relationship with Baresi remains intact."

"I appreciate that."

"And your daughter can come to me at any time for help if she needs it." He glanced at Gabi and grinned, shooting a dart of sunlight into her soul. "Though she probably won't. She's smart and she's stubborn. And hopefully she now knows that she's worth more than anyone has ever given her credit for."

Oh, dear heavens. It was like he'd been dropped, completely perfect, into her lap. Once again, she was reminded of the fact that she never seemed to meet the right guy at the right time. Either the timing was wrong or the man was. Having him on her side but not being with him was going to be torturous. And yet she wasn't in any position to turn him away. He was too valuable an ally, in business but mostly in friendship.

Gabi hugged her father again. "Are you angry with me, Papa?"

He chuckled. "I don't know what to say. It seems so unreal and… I don't know. But I'm not angry. I'm sorry you ever felt you needed to go to such lengths."

"I'd do anything for you, Papa. You know that."

"And I'd do the same for you, and your sister, and your mama." He squeezed her tight. "This isn't going to beat me. I'm going to fight it. So please don't worry."

She nodded against his chest. Why had she worried so much? Her father had always been willing to forgive any transgression. She shouldn't have taken this burden on alone.

"You should get some rest before you have to leave for the hospital. And I'm going to pack a bag. I'll be staying at my flat."

"I'll drive you," Will said. "I need to return the rental, anyway, and I want to make sure everyone is all right before I fly back to Paris."

Paris. Of course he would be leaving now. The

tabloids had quieted, no one had come looking for her, and Will had to know by now that she had no intention of spilling the actual story to the press. Because he trusted her.

Oh, she was going to miss him.

"It looks as though everything is sorted," Lucia said. "Massimo and I are leaving around three."

"Mama, you can stay with me at my flat if you like."

Lucia shook her head. "*Grazie*, but I am going to stay with Zia Isabella. She lives closer to the hospital, and I haven't seen her in a while."

Will rose from his chair. "If that's the case, I should go upstairs and wrap up some business I was working on. Signor and Signora Baresi, thank you for your hospitality the past few days." He held out his hand to Massimo. "And the best of luck to you tomorrow."

"You are welcome here anytime," Massimo replied, shaking Will's hand.

He left and went toward the stairs, and Gabi waited until she heard his footsteps above her. Then she let out a huge breath.

Lucia looked at her with a crooked smile and a raised eyebrow. "Any hope there?" she asked. "Of the real kind?"

Gabi shook her head. "No. It's too messy." She met her mother's gaze. "But I'm a bit sorry about that."

She stood on tiptoe and kissed her father's

cheek. "I'll see you before you go," she said softly. "And again tomorrow at the hospital."

"Ti amo, gattina," he said, kissing her cheek in return.

She escaped to the stairs before he could see the tears in her eyes. No one had ever loved her as unconditionally as her parents. They loved each other the same way.

Why had Gabi ever even considered that she could settle for anything less?

CHAPTER NINE

WILLIAM KNEW HE should hop on a plane and fly back to Paris. It would be the smart thing to do at this point, and it was what was expected. He'd had a sharply worded email from Stephen, and another from his mother that was less angry and more concerned. Why was he still in Italy? He should forget about Gabriella Baresi now that the media story seemed under control, and get back home and to work. The family, who'd congregated at the manor for the wedding, were now all back in either London or Paris for work, and he should be, too. According to Aurora Germain Pemberton, anyway.

But he couldn't leave yet. Not while Gabi was sitting with her mother and sister, waiting while Massimo was having surgery to have a section of his colon removed. Marco was there, too, and right now had gone to get coffee for everyone. Will found he quite liked the younger man, who seemed bright and energetic but now, at a serious time, stepped up and provided support for

Giulia. According to Gabi, they'd been seeing each other off and on for some time, though it had only recently become a steady thing.

He went to the chairs in the waiting area and sat down beside Gabi. "How're you holding up?"

"Okay. It's taking so long."

He knew. The surgeon had estimated the surgery to take about ninety minutes, and then of course Massimo would be taken to recovery. But it was already five in the afternoon. It had been three hours already, and no doctor, no word.

Of course everyone was thinking the worst. Were there complications? More cancer than they realized? Had it spread?

Will's father had died suddenly, from a heart attack. There'd been no waiting around for results, no hope. One minute Cedric had been alive, then next he was gone. It had been excruciating, but watching the Baresi women worry, he wasn't sure this was a better alternative. He hoped that it all worked out right in the end, and Massimo would be going home again.

Marco returned with coffee and a bag of pastries for everyone to share. "You need to eat something, Mama Lucia," he said, pressing a paper napkin and a sweet into her hand.

"*Grazie*, Marco," she whispered, but Will saw that her face was pale and her eyes dull with worry.

Will leaned over and whispered in Gabi's ear. "Eat one, and maybe your mother will, too."

She nodded, then looked up at Marco. "I'll have one, thank you."

Giulia rose and put her arms around Marco's waist. "Thank you for being here with us."

"I wouldn't be anywhere else, *cara*."

Gabi nibbled on her bun and Will sat back, sipping on strong coffee, wishing the doctors would hurry up.

Gabi had been a wreck. Not outwardly, of course, but he'd noticed how quiet she'd been. Last night, after Lucia and Massimo had left for the hospital, she'd barely eaten. Instead she'd gone into the library to work for a while, she'd said. Giulia had come home and they'd spoken for a bit, and Will had been the one to venture into the kitchen and throw something together for dinner and make sure she ate. It was the same this morning, before they'd left for Perugia. He'd made sure she'd eaten breakfast so she had something in her stomach to get her through the day.

He knew how he'd feel if this were his mother, or any of his siblings. He'd be sick with worry and waiting. So he sat beside her and when she tilted her neck to release tension, he put his hand on her back and gently rubbed, trying to help ease the muscles.

"I'm glad you're here," she murmured.

"Me, too. I could have flown back today but I would have worried the whole time." He tried a smile. "Who would have thought that I'd stick around for moral support, huh?"

She smiled back. "When I opened that hotel room door in London and you were there, you looked ready to kill."

"I was angry."

"You had a right to be."

"I wasn't angry for long. I think I stopped about the time you fell asleep on the plane."

"I wanted to be angry with you, too, but I knew you were trying to help. It was a lot of hating you for bossing me around and knowing I deserved it because it was my fault."

He nodded, then started to chuckle a bit. "It was a pretty unorthodox way to get to know each other. But…" He looked up at her and the connection between them was strong and sure. "I don't regret it. Not a moment."

"Me, either. I appreciate you trying to help with Stephen, too. But don't worry about Baresi. I'm going to figure everything out."

"I know you will. Now eat. You need something since you refused lunch."

The coffee was gone and the pastries half-eaten and discarded when finally, finally, the doctor came through the doors toward the family.

Everyone stood together.

"The surgery went well, though not without complication," he said, not mincing any words. "The tumor was a bit bigger than we anticipated, and Signor Baresi had some bleeding that we needed to get under control, which extended the length of the surgery. We removed lymph nodes that we'll send for testing to see if the cancer has spread."

The family seemed to be collectively holding their breath.

"But overall it was a success. He'll be in recovery for some time, and access is restricted."

"The bleeding…was it serious?"

The surgeon looked at Giulia, who'd asked the question. "Serious enough, but he's a strong man and healthy for his age. I don't anticipate further postoperative problems, but we'll wait and see."

He looked at the rest of the group. "He's going to be on some pretty strong pain medication. It'd be better for you to try to see him tomorrow. I understand you'll want to wait to see him, though, Signora Baresi."

He said his goodbyes and left. Will sensed the collective relief of the family as if they had all let out a giant breath. "Well, that's good news," he said, and he looked over at Gabi. She looked ready to drop, so he put his arm around her shoulders and pulled her to his side. "First hurdle over, yes?"

She nodded, and he saw she was blinking quickly. His heart melted a little and he turned her into his arms. "It's okay now," he said gently, rubbing her back. "He made it through the surgery. You can breathe again."

He looked over and saw Marco holding Giulia's hand and Lucia watching William and Gabi with tenderness lining her face. His feelings were so transparent, weren't they? He really did need to get back to Paris, before he did something foolish.

But not tonight. Right now Gabi was crying softly into his chest and he would make sure she was all right and that Massimo got through the night okay. As long as everything went well, William would be on a flight from Rome to Paris tomorrow afternoon, back in his flat tomorrow night and in the office on Thursday.

It sounded horrid and dull, and he rather suspected it was because she wouldn't be there.

"Come, now," he said softly, rubbing her shoulder. "It's all right. Your mama is going to stay and be with him when he's awake. You need some food and some rest."

She nodded against him, and lifted her chin as she pulled away. "Sorry. I think the relief hit me."

"It's no problem."

Gabi looked at her sister and said, "Do you and Marco want to stay at my flat tonight? I have room."

Giulia looked at Marco, and then back at Gabi. "Marco and I are going to drive home. But we'll be back tomorrow. The drive isn't that long. Call if there's anything…" Her lip quivered. "You know."

Marco nodded. "I'll have her back here in no time."

"Whatever you want," Gabi said. "Mama?"

"I'm staying with your father, but I'll go to Isabella's later."

"Promise you'll take care of yourself. I can stay with you…"

"No," Lucia said firmly. "Will is right. I bet you hardly slept last night. Go home. You're only minutes away and I will call if there's a change. But I am fine, I promise. Now that he's through the surgery, I'm fine." She smiled tiredly. "Now we fight."

"Oh, Mama, I love you," Gabi said, and she went for a hug.

Will waited while everyone said their goodbyes, and told Lucia to give Massimo their love. By the time they finally left the hospital, it was nearly eight p.m. Will had awakened at six that morning and had heard Gabi already up and about. She had to be ready to drop by now.

"Let's get you home, and then I'll head to a hotel," he said. "You need sleep."

Gabi looked up at him and shook her head. "You don't need a hotel. I have a spare room. You can stay with me, and go straight to the airport tomorrow. If you want to."

And just like that she'd put the decision on

him. He knew what he wanted and knew what he should do and they weren't the same thing at all. Sleeping in her spare room, knowing she was there, too, in a bed alone, was a torturous thought. Going to a lonely hotel was no better.

"Let's get you home first and maybe some actual dinner, and then we'll see."

Once outside she took a deep breath and let it out, as if shaking off the weight of the world. She rolled her shoulders a bit. "Do you want me to drive?" she asked. "I know the city. My flat is about ten minutes away."

"Sure, if you want to." He dug in his pocket for the keys, and before long Gabi was behind the wheel, navigating her way out of the hospital and through the city streets.

It seemed no time at all before she pulled up in front of a building and parked on the street. "This is me," she said, looking up at a nondescript three-story building with affection. "My flat is the top two floors. I got lucky with it. The neighborhood is quiet and lovely, and it's a nice walk to the historic center. The offices are on the other side of the city, so I drive or take transit. But I fell in love with this place and I've lived here for four years, ever since I started working at Baresi."

He got out and started to open the back door for his bag, when she said, "No, wait. Before we go up, I need food. I haven't been home in weeks.

The cupboard is most definitely bare and there's nothing in the refrigerator. Leave your bag. We'll only be a few minutes."

It was only a short walk to a street with a smattering of cafés, a few markets and one pizzeria that smelled heavenly. "You can get pizza if you want," she said, "but my favorite thing of all is their *porchetta* sandwiches. Let's get the basics first and come back."

At the market they stocked up on coffee, bread, butter and, at Will's insistence, eggs. "I'm dying for a mess of eggs," he confessed. "I could make you an omelet. I need cheese, and good ham—"

"You're in the right part of Italy for good ham," she replied, and their basket got fuller. Tomatoes and mushrooms followed, and Gabi insisted on truffles, and then there was wine. By the time they paid, they were both carrying two bags each.

"Now for sandwiches," she said, and they popped into the pizzeria. Will stood back while she talked and joked in Italian with the young man behind the counter. He could only pick up a few words, because they were speaking so fast, but he didn't mind. Gabi's face was relaxed and animated. She'd needed to come home, he realized. Not just to the villa but to the home she'd made for herself. For the first time, he felt like he was finally seeing the real Gabi, and he liked her even more. This was her neighborhood and these were her people. They knew her and liked her. A young woman, very pregnant, came around the counter and gave her a hug. Will picked up enough Italian to know she asked about Massimo, and Gabi answered briefly.

The young man handed over a bag of sandwiches and then a separate bag with a wink. When Gabi protested, he waved his hands and walked away. *"Grazie!"* she called out, and then they were headed to the door again.

"What's in the other bag?" Will asked as they stepped outside again.

"Tiramisu that Bianca made this morning. Bianca is his wife. Expecting their third baby any day now. I probably eat there more than I should, but..."

He nudged her elbow. "They're your friends. It's lovely. Remember that curry place I told you about? I felt the same way. I walked in and it felt like being welcomed into their family."

"It's nice, isn't it?"

"Very."

They were already back at her door. "Let's take this up first, and come back for the bags."

He followed her up the stairs to the third floor. There was no elevator, but he didn't mind. She unlocked her door and they stepped inside. It was hot; the windows had been shut up while she was gone, and as soon as she put her bags on the counter, she went to the French doors and opened them to reveal a small balcony. Fresh air rushed into the flat. "Phew, that's better," she said. "It's stuffy in here."

It was lovely. He remembered she'd said the flat was two floors. What he could see was a small but well-equipped kitchen, an airy living space with a sofa and two chairs and a small powder room off to one side. "How many bedrooms?" he asked, curious. It was really quite a lovely space.

"Two," she replied, opening the refrigerator. She put the tiramisu inside, and then started to put away the perishables from the market. "I have the extra for Giulia or Mama and Papa."

"Your father...he commutes?"

"Yes. But the offices are closer to the villa than we are now."

"They sold the house in town for financial reasons, right?"

Gabi paused and met his gaze. "Yes. Not as an emergency, but as a way of...streamlining. But I can't be sorry they kept the villa. It will always be the first place I think of when I think of home."

He wiggled his fingers for the keys. "You do this, and I'll get the bags. I'm starving."

She nodded and handed them over. Will jogged down the stairs and retrieved their bags. Gabi's suitcase was huge, and by the time he reached the top he was breathing heavily.

Gabi laughed at him when he stepped inside, and he grinned. "What do you have in here, bricks?"

"It's what I had at Chatsworth and what I was taking on my honeymoon. I really don't keep my things at the villa. Here, sit down outside and I'll bring you the best sandwich you've ever eaten."

He was expecting wine, since she seemed to prefer it, so he was surprised when she brought the sandwich on a plate and a cold beer to drink.

It was perfect in its simplicity. Crusty bread, sliced pork…and nothing else. But the *porchetta* was like nothing he'd ever eaten. There were flavors of rosemary and then the crispy skin and the tender flesh that all combined into something extraordinary.

"Oh. I get it now."

She grinned, the smile spreading from ear to ear. "See? I told you."

"This is amazing. How do you not eat this every day?"

She laughed. "I like vegetables. But I won't lie, I buy one of Gio's sandwiches once a week as a treat."

He took two more bites and the gnawing in his stomach started to ease. He sat back a bit and toyed with his beer bottle, and looked at the view. "This is incredible. You can see so much of the city from up here."

"I fell in love with it," she said quietly. "It was

the view that sold me. I don't need a large place for just me, but I stepped out here and took a deep breath and that was it. It's an entirely different view, but it reminds me of looking down over the valley from the olive groves at the villa. It felt familiar, and I liked that."

"It's the feeling, not the actual view," he said, understanding. "It's how I feel in the orchard at the château."

"You mean at the bench where we…" She blushed a little and turned away. "You took me there on purpose, didn't you?"

"I needed the calm and I thought you did, too. Caused us some bother, though, didn't it?"

She laughed. "You know, if someone took a photo of us now, I don't think I'd mind as much as I did then."

He took another drink of beer, met her gaze and said, "Me, either."

They were quiet for long minutes, finishing their sandwiches, enjoying the solitude, not feeling compelled to make conversation. It was comfortable. Wonderful. William had never experienced anything like it in his life. Not with any of the women he'd dated or in any relationship. He'd always felt he had to be "on." Sparkling conversation. Endless charm. This being easy and comfortable with each other was new and he liked it. A lot.

Gabi got up, took their plates and went inside.

When she came back, she had the dessert with her and two forks. He really didn't need sweets, but it looked too gorgeous to turn away.

Gabi tasted hers, then said, "So, I haven't asked you this before, but…there's no girlfriend, is there?"

His head lifted sharply. "What? No. Of course not. I wouldn't have…especially at the villa…if there were."

"I'm sorry. I didn't mean to offend you."

"You didn't. Surprised me, yes. But considering your last relationship—Stephen not included—you have a right to ask."

"Do I? What right? We're friends. That's all."

He wasn't sure he was ready for this conversation. He should have flown home. Avoided this whole thing. Because he was probably going to have to lie to her, and he hated that. Still, after Stephen's abrupt departure, Will really didn't want to create a big rift in the family. Not when they were already fragmented by his father's death.

"Gabi…we both know this is more complicated than either of us like. Not just the situation, but… feelings." He was stopping and starting so much he figured he sounded like an idiot. "Maybe I should get a hotel for tonight."

Her eyes widened. "What if I don't want you to get a hotel?"

Her question surprised him. "What are you suggesting? We established that we were friends—"

"Even you can't fool yourself into believing that," she interrupted, twisting her fingers together on the tabletop. "This isn't easy for me, either. But tomorrow you are leaving. We both know it. You have a life to get back to, and Papa…he's through his surgery. I have a company to run and so do you. But tonight…"

She turned quite red as she chanced a look up at him. "Tonight you're here. And no one else is."

"Gabi…"

"If you don't want to, that's fine. We'll part as friends and that will be that. But if you do…want to, that is, I—I'm…" She was stuttering a bit now, nervous and insecure. She shouldn't be. He couldn't remember ever wanting a woman more.

"No one needs to know," she finished. "I mean, we can be discreet."

It felt like sneaking around, hiding things, when in reality he wished it were different and they could try being together. "And then what?" he asked, his voice hoarse. He didn't know why he was giving her a reason to change her mind, other than he wanted her to be very sure this was what she wanted.

He did. So very much. It wasn't just that she was beautiful, though she was. It was how she loved her family. How she stood up to Stephen. Even the warmth and grace with which she spoke to her neighbors. He liked her as a person, desired her as a woman.

"I don't want you to have any regrets," he said.

"My only regret would be letting you walk away tomorrow without taking this chance." Her voice was soft and rode over his nerve endings like silk. "It isn't just chemistry, Will. You're the right kind of man at the wrong time, but at least I might be able to keep the memory of a wonderful night."

"Gabi," he replied, knowing she would have her way. Why not, when it was what he wanted, too? He was tired of the heavy weight of his loyalty dragging him down. She was right. She was also the right kind of woman at the wrong time, and he wished with all his heart that he might have met her first. But he hadn't, and so if tonight was all they'd have, he'd make sure it was a memory worth keeping.

Were they being crazy? Reckless? Probably. Was it a bad thing? Maybe, maybe not. After their kisses against the olive tree, he'd known this was what he wanted. "Here," he said, tapping his lap. "I want to hold you in my arms and watch the sun disappear."

"Oh, Will…"

"We have time, Gabi. If this is our only night, I don't want to rush it."

Gabi perched on his knee, then leaned back against his shoulder. The evening air was cooling but Will was so perfectly warm. His right arm came around her, holding her in place. The light was soft as it touched the trees, gaps in the green tops punctuated by ancient buildings in the town's historic center.

This was her favorite place on a summer evening, and to share it with Will made it even more special.

He was so unexpected. So perfect. But she tried to imagine walking into a Pemberton family function on his arm and knew it was impossible. This really was all they had, and she wanted to soak in every precious second.

His fingers grazed down her arm, stroking back and forth, as she pointed out the general area of landmarks like the Arco Etrusco and the Piazza IV Novembre. How she wished she could keep him to herself for a few days, walk the cobbled streets, take him to the gallery. Show him the city she called home. An emptiness opened up inside, knowing it could never be what she wanted.

She couldn't think that way, not now. They must embrace and enjoy every moment they had together.

"Is it strange that just sitting like this is wonderful?" he murmured, his lips close to her ear.

Goose bumps rose on her arms at the warmth of his breath on her neck. "I was thinking the same thing. It's as close to perfect as I can think of right now."

He shifted, so her knees were over his lap and her arm was around his neck. "Gabi, these last two weeks—not even—have been the craziest and best I have ever had. How is that even possible?" He shook his head with wonder. "I was so angry with you, and then I admired you, and then I couldn't stop thinking about you."

"I know," she answered. "I feel the same. And I felt so wrong, too. Because you're Stephen's brother. I was supposed to be the problem and you were supposed to be the enemy, and honestly, after about twenty minutes I couldn't think of you that way."

"My brother's a damned fool."

"Let's make that the last time we mention your brother tonight, shall we?" She curled in closer. "Tonight is about you and me. Only you and me."

And then Gabi leaned forward and touched her lips to his, something they hadn't done since the olive grove.

He tasted like beer and hints of espresso and cream from the tiramisu, and a particular flavor that was just Will. His lips opened and invited her in, and she made a little noise of surrender as she pressed herself closer, looping her knees over the arm of the chair and wrapping her other hand around his neck. He leaned forward a little, bracing her back with one strong arm, and deepened the kiss.

And still he didn't hurry. Instead they took

their time, kissing on her balcony, letting the lights of Perugia come on, blinking and twinkling as darkness settled.

His hand slid out of her hair and over her shoulder, then down over her breast.

"Mmm." She arched into his palm, loving the sensation. "That feels so good."

In response, his thumb flicked over her nipple, and she gasped into his mouth. "Will…"

"We should go inside, before we give your neighbors a free show," he suggested.

She knew he was right. Once inside, she led him through the flat to the stairs, and began the climb to her bedroom. The air was warmer as they approached the second floor, and once inside her bedroom, she went to the window, opening it wide to let in the cooling air.

"I'm sorry it's so warm," she apologized.

"Don't be. It'll be cooler with our clothes off." He grinned at her again, and she figured her whole body flushed at his suggestion. Goodness, she wasn't some green virgin. Why did he have the power to embarrass her so?

"Are you nervous, Gabriella?"

"A little."

"Me, too."

"Why are you nervous?" she asked.

"We may only have tonight," he said, "but it feels important, don't you think? I don't want to screw it up."

"Oh, Will. You couldn't. I promise." She went to him. "You're the most decent man I've ever met. You're handsome and sexy and kind and funny and you make me crazy. I want to touch you everywhere and have you touch me. I want you to kiss me like you never want to stop. I want you to make love to me, Will. Because I trust you. I trust you with me, and that isn't something that happens very often."

Especially not now, after living a lie for so long. But Will…he was different. She knew it deep inside, where it mattered.

He didn't answer. He gathered her in his arms for a passionate kiss that emptied her brain of anything but him. She fumbled with the buttons of his shirt; he pulled her top over her head, leaving her standing in her bra and trousers. Wordlessly she reached for the button and zip on her pants and let them drop to the floor, stepping out of them to stand before him in lacy peekaboo panties that matched the bra. His nostrils flared as he looked at her, his eyes glowing in the twilight of the room. Then he undid the button of his jeans and took them off, so he was standing in a pair of dark boxer briefs.

"Touch me, then," he invited, and she closed the distance between them in a nanosecond. His breath hissed as she pressed against him, skin to skin, and cupped him in her hand.

"God," he groaned. "I didn't expect that."

"I'm not shy," she replied, moving her hand. "I want all of this, Will. I want to give and I want to take. Oh, your skin is so warm." Her abdomen grazed his, and she marveled at the beautiful feeling of skin against skin. Was there anything sexier?

For a while they took their time exploring, touching here, kissing there, learning what the other liked, where the sensitive spots were. He reached behind her and unclasped her bra with one hand, and she wrapped her arms around his neck so that she was pressed firmly against him. She couldn't get enough of that feeling. There were no barriers between them, not physically and not emotionally, either. Gabi couldn't remember a time when she'd been this naked with someone. She'd been too afraid. Too worried about trying to be "right." She didn't worry about that with Will. He seemed to want her just as she was.

He scooped her up in his arms and carried her the short distance to the bed, then laid her down and stretched out beside her, on his side so that his left hand made trails over her breasts, her belly, the tiny bit of fabric between her legs. He braced his weight on his right arm and let his lips follow the path of his hand, until she wasn't sure how much more she could stand.

When she thought she might weep or else somehow come out of her skin with wanting, he shed his briefs and skimmed her panties down her legs. "In the drawer," she whispered, turning her head to look at the small stand beside the bed. "There should be a condom in there."

He opened the drawer and found the tiny foil packet. Then there was nothing holding them back. They met equally and enthusiastically. If Gabi were only going to have this one chance to be with him, she wanted to make it something to remember.

There was no particular rush; once Will paused and gripped the pillows beside her head, clenching his teeth. "Not yet," he ground out. "I want it to last."

"Mmm, me, too," she answered, but subtly moved her hips, teasing, tempting. She wasn't ready for it to be over, either, but there was something alluring about challenging his control.

"Minx," he growled, and the next thing she knew he had pulled out and slid down her body, taking revenge. She could hardly breathe as he loved her with his mouth, and she cried out, saying his name as she climaxed.

She was still sensitive and pulsing when he slid into her again, and this time he didn't hold back. Their skin grew slick in the heat, and she tasted salt under her tongue as she kissed his shoulder. A bead of sweat dropped from his forehead to her breast, and when he finally came, he growled out her full name—Gabriella—and held her gaze, making her heart tremble. It couldn't be more clear that they hadn't just made love but they'd made love to each other. It was more than sex and desire. To Gabi, it was as if all the missing pieces of her life clicked into place when she was in his arms.

And in a matter of hours he was walking away.

Will caught his breath, collapsing on the bed beside her. "Well, damn."

She laughed. "I was thinking the same thing."

"Give me a minute." He got up and disappeared into her bathroom, then came back again, stark naked.

Gabi rested on an elbow, admired him as he walked back to the bed and said, "Now that's a better view than the one from my balcony."

"I'm glad you think so."

"You're making fun of me."

"No, I'm just happy. Tonight I'm going to let myself be happy. Tomorrow is enough time to worry about…what I need to worry about."

"Cleaning up messes?"

He chuckled, lying down beside her so they were face-to-face. "This time I get to clean up my own mess. This wasn't supposed to happen."

"I know. None of it was, Will. Maybe I should be sorry, but I'm not."

"Me, either."

"I wish…" She halted, wondering if it was

right to put what she was feeling into words, but knowing if she didn't she'd probably regret it. "I wish I had met you first. Your brother is angry with me right now, but I know he's a good man underneath. We didn't have this kind of connection, though."

"I'm glad." Will's face darkened. "It's selfish of me, I know. But I'm glad it wasn't like this with him. And yet..." He sighed. "This still feels like a betrayal."

"Because he's your brother. And even if I didn't break his heart, I hurt him just the same. And your loyalty is to family. I understand, you know. I do."

"I'm glad, because I'm not sure I understand."

She thought for a moment, then smiled softly. "I remember this American show I watched a few years ago, and they were talking about the 'bro code.' It was between best friends but I understood. There are just some things that you don't do to a friend or brother. I'm pretty sure this would qualify. So I do understand. I'm just going to miss you."

"I'm going to miss you, too." He traced a fingertip over her arm. The room was still warm, the summer air caressing their skin, and Gabi had no desire to get under the covers. Right now her legs were twined with Will's, her hand resting on his rib cage. There was nowhere else she would rather be.

He looked into her eyes. "Will you let me know how your father is?"

Why did he have to be so caring? Didn't he have any flaws whatsoever? For a moment she hesitated, a cold thought settling in her stomach. What if he wasn't this perfect? What if she was missing something?

"What is it?" he asked, frowning. "What's wrong?"

"Nothing," she answered, pushing the thought away. "And of course I'll let you know about Papa. It seems a little selfish that he's in the hospital tonight and we're here. Until this moment, I hadn't given him a thought."

"You're allowed a little time to yourself, you know. You've been worrying about him constantly."

"Would you mind if I checked my messages? He should be out of recovery by now."

"Of course."

She slid off the bed and grabbed a light robe from the back of her door before slipping into the kitchen and grabbing the phone off the counter. She pressed the button and it lit up in the dark. Sure enough, there was a text from her mother that she'd sent to both Gabi and Giulia.

Papa is awake and in his room. He is very groggy but doing well. Please get some sleep and we will see you tomorrow.

Get some sleep. Gabi thought of the man currently in her room and wondered if they'd sleep much at all. And even if they did, she knew she'd lie awake, wishing, wanting things she couldn't have.

But it didn't matter, anyway. The responsibility of Baresi was on her shoulders right now. That had to be her focus. Her personal life—what there was of it—could wait.

CHAPTER TEN

THE LAST THING Will wanted to do the next day was get on a plane and fly to Paris. But here he was, sitting in the airport in Rome, waiting for his flight, missing Gabi already.

Ten days. They'd spent ten days together and already his life felt permanently altered.

This morning had been torture. Oh, Gabi had put a good face on it. She'd made coffee while he'd cooked her an omelet, and they'd made love one last time before he'd jumped in her shower and dressed for the flight.

He'd left her at her door, both of them trying to smile, but he'd seen the brightness in her eyes as he'd prepared to say goodbye. It was amazing to him that she cared about him that much.

In the end he'd said nothing, just dropped a light kiss on her lips and turned to walk away, straight to the car. He'd had to get away, out of sight, so he'd driven three blocks before pulling over and setting up the GPS so he could find his way to the airport.

And if his eyes had been misty, too, then so be it. Maybe he was the guy who cleaned up the messes and lived on the straight and narrow these days, but he still had feelings, dammit. And he cared for her a lot. If fate was really a thing, it seemed a cruel joke that he met her too late.

For a while he'd wondered if the attraction had been because she was exactly the wrong person. In earlier years, he'd made those foolish decisions, and he'd caught himself at times over the last week and a half, wondering if he was falling into old patterns.

But he was not. It wasn't that Gabi was dangerous and risky, or that she fit some sort of rebellion against the family. Those days were gone. He cared about her because she was, quite simply, wonderful.

His flight was called and he went to the gate, then boarded and found his business-class seat. The in-flight Wi-Fi meant he could start catching up on the work emails he'd missed the past two days. He might as well get stuck in the thick of things. It was probably the best way to forget.

It was raining in Paris when he landed, and the car service took him from the airport to his apartment in the heart of the city. He loved Paris, perhaps even more than London, maybe because he'd spent so much time here as a child as his parents built Aurora, Inc., into the massive enterprise it was today. Even in the rain Paris was beautiful, with its shiny pavement and magical streets.

His apartment was a sprawling thing, with a wall of windows overlooking the river. He dropped his bag and went to the windows, looking out over the city he called home, and thought about all the times he had stood with Gabi in special places. In the lemon grove, on top of the hill at the villa, last night on her balcony. Places that resonated with them both, and he wished he could share this one with her now.

But she was back in Perugia, getting on with her life, and he was in France, doing the same.

But damn, he missed her.

He sent an email to the family announcing his return and then went to his bedroom to unpack as his phone started blowing up with requests for meetings.

The old routine, back again.

But he sighed and looked out the windows again at the glistening, wet streets. It was different now because he was different. And all the keeping busy in the world wouldn't change it.

Gabi was used to being front and center in the financial aspects of Baresi Textiles, but in the days that followed her father's surgery, she found herself in the midst of the full-on operations of the company. To say she was overwhelmed was an understatement, but the employees all knew her well. For the most part, everyone was helpful and asked about Massimo's recovery daily.

As she sat at her desk, wading through emails, she realized that her father had built a company where the employees were contented and invested. That was saying something. She owed it to them to do a good job now. Captain the ship in his absence. And ask for help when she needed it.

After three days of back and forth with one of their main accounts, though, she felt she needed some advice. Massimo was at home and still on pain medication; once he'd healed sufficiently he'd start a grueling chemotherapy regime. She could ask him. Thought she probably should, but didn't. Instead she sent an email and sat back in her chair, wondering if she'd done the right thing.

Five minutes later her phone rang.

"Hi," she said, thrilled at the fast response, anxious to hear his voice again.

"God, it's good to hear your voice," he said, and she thrilled at the sound, so deep and soft.

"Oh, you, too. Things are okay in Paris?"

"Busy but fine. And you? You said you want my opinion on something."

She hesitated. She was about to reveal things about her business that made her vulnerable. But he'd also said if she needed help or advice to call him. It came down to trust, didn't it? And though she'd had misgivings at first, she trusted him. He hadn't done one single thing to make her think otherwise.

"It's one of our clients, actually. He's been with us for over fifteen years, but now he's making noise about not renewing his contract."

"Any particular reason?"

She sighed and pinched the bridge of her nose. "He says it's because he can get the same quality product cheaper elsewhere, but I don't think that's it. It's no secret that Papa is ill. I think he's worried that the company will be in trouble without Papa here. That he doesn't trust…current management."

"I'd laugh if I didn't think it was absolutely possible. Some people's opinions are still archaic. But really, what it comes down to is trust. Trust in your product and trust in you. Not Massimo, but you."

"But I've been doing this job for ten minutes. Know what I mean? How do I get him to trust me?"

Will's voice was warm in her ear. "You go see him, in person. You remind him that you grew up in this company, that you've worked in the family business and that you're completely capable of sitting in that chair while your father is taking care of his health. You look him in the eye and shake his hand. And you go armed with quality samples and numbers. Make sure he knows you've done your homework. A face-to-face meeting can change everything."

"You make it sound so easy."

Will laughed. "Oh, it's not. But you have to learn how. If you're going to sit in the big chair you have to be worthy of it. What would your father do?"

Gabi let out a breath, knowing he was right. "He'd go see him in person."

"Now you're getting it."

"But…what if I do all that and he's still determined to leave? It's a big contract, Will. If we lose it, it'll hit us hard."

Will sighed. "Sometimes that happens, too. Sometimes despite our best efforts, we fail. And so we pick ourselves up and find other solutions. You can do this, Gabi. I have faith in you."

"More than I have in myself, obviously. But thank you for the advice. I needed some common sense, I think."

"Of course." He paused and then his voice softened. "And how's your father? Doing better?"

"Home from the hospital, and thank you for asking. He's cranky at not being able to do much, which is an improvement from before the surgery, because he was too tired and not his old self. The more he drives Mama crazy, the more relieved she is."

Will chuckled and then sighed. "And you? How are you? Other than working all the time?"

"I'm fine." But the truth was, she was lonely. And not lonely in general—lonely for him in particular. "And you?"

"If 'fine' is the same as missing you, then I'm fine as well."

"Oh, Will." Still, his words lit something inside her. She'd needed to hear them desperately. To know that the ache left in her chest wasn't hers alone.

"I miss you, Gabi."

"I miss you, too. Crazy when you think about it, but...yeah."

"I'm terribly glad you emailed. I like to think that we're friends. That you know I'm here for you if you need something."

There was that word again...*friends*. They'd used it after the kisses in the olive grove, and for a few whole days they'd managed to not act on their desires. Until they were faced with parting. Then those cautions and assurances had gone right out the window. She probably should regret it, but she never would.

"I like that, too, Will. Everything is okay there? I keep watching the magazines and internet, but I haven't seen anything recently. It looks as though it's forgotten."

"There was a brief mention somewhere about Stephen visiting you...that we might have planted. No one wants to read about rescheduling the wedding. They want a scandal."

"If they only knew," she said, and laughed a little. His warm chuckle came across the line and she closed her eyes, wishing she could hear it in person.

"I've got a meeting in five minutes, but I hope that helped," he said, and she felt a bit of letdown knowing their conversation was coming to an end.

"It did. Sometimes it just feels as if I'm doing this alone. Your advice has given me some confidence, so thank you."

"Will you call and let me know how it goes?"

"If you want me to."

"I do, Gabi. There's no reason why we have to stop talking to each other."

Wasn't there? They weren't going to be together. They both knew it. It hadn't even been on the table as an option. And yet hearing his voice today was like having a lifeline, something to keep her going when she got overwhelmed with the responsibilities in front of her. She didn't want to let her father down, or anyone else for that matter.

"Then I'll let you know how it goes. Good or bad."

"I'm sure it'll be fine. I believe in you."

Oh, great. Another person she didn't want to disappoint.

"Thank you, Will. Go to your meeting. I'm fine."

"Take care, Gabi."

"You, too."

She hung up the phone and sat back in her chair. Was she torturing herself by talking to Will? Could they possibly be just friends?

Two days later she was in Milan, as nervous as she'd ever been, waiting to see Giacomo Corsetti. Giacomo had been her father's client for a decade and a half. The Corsetti brand was more high street fashion than couture, but it prided itself on exceptional quality. Gabi had dressed to impress: a splendidly cut pantsuit in navy and off-white, matching shoes and a designer bag that held several reports and an iPad so she could bring up data in real time if she needed. She'd put up her hair—more businesslike—and been subtle with her makeup. Overall she was going for a stylish but competent look.

If only her insides were as confident as the outside looked.

"Gabriella!" A jovial voice echoed across the marble floor and she turned to see Giacomo approaching. He wasn't overly tall, and his mustache was grayer than when she'd last seen him. "*Buongiorno*, Gabriella. How good it is to see you." He came forward and kissed both cheeks, making her realize that he was, indeed, a good inch or two shorter than she was. Perhaps the heels were a mistake.

"It's good to see you, too, Giacomo." She smiled at him.

"Last time I saw you, you were starting university. You've grown up a lot."

She had to dispel the image of her as a child, so she held her smile and replied, "Yes, I have. I've been working with the company for several years now."

"Learning at the elbow of the master?"

"Just as you say. It made perfect sense for me to step in as Papa is recovering."

Giacomo gestured toward the hall, and they began walking, Gabi's heels clicking on the cool marble. "How is your father? Such a sad thing, the cancer."

"He's doing well. He's home from surgery and starts chemo in a few weeks. The prognosis is encouraging." She looked over at Giacomo and added, "He looks far better now than he did before the operation, in fact."

"I'm very glad to hear it."

He led her into a large office in a modern design. For all his old-school attitudes, Giacomo knew how to keep up with what was fashionable. He went to sit behind a large desk, but Gabi halted and swept out a hand. "I have some figures to show you. Why don't we sit at your table where we can spread them out?"

If he sat behind his desk and she in front of

it, she'd feel like a naughty student in the principal's office.

"Of course, of course."

Once they were seated she proceeded to take out her spreadsheets and make her case. Giacomo listened politely, but when she was finished, he tapped his fingers on the table.

"You see, Gabriella, I can get product much cheaper elsewhere."

"Ah, but it's not Baresi quality. Corsetti has always prided itself on its quality. What is it you say? Couture quality at high street prices?"

"The market is changing."

She hesitated for a moment, then met his gaze. "Yes, it is shifting, which is why I outlined some options for a new contract, to give you some flexibility. We want to work *with* you, Giacomo. What's good for Corsetti is good for Baresi."

"I'd have to be able to source at a lower price." He named a number that was bordering on insulting. In fact, it was insulting considering their long history of doing business together. To concede to such a price would obliterate any profit margin for Baresi.

"Come now, Giacomo. You know that's not possible. If you're trying to negotiate up, that's a very low place to start." She held his gaze. The whole time she was thinking, *What would Will do?* She knew he'd stand his ground and do what was right for Aurora. And so would she.

"It is my offer," he said firmly.

Gabi started to get mad now. Did he think she was stupid? She gathered up her papers to give herself time to decide what to say. Finally she folded her hands on top of the table, looked him in the eyes and said, "If my father were sitting here, you would never have asked such a thing. We both know it."

"*Signorina—*" he started, but she lifted a hand.

"No, Giacomo. I am the head of Baresi Textiles right now. I am young and I am a woman, but I am not green. You know my father. You know he would not have entrusted this responsibility to me if he did not think I was fully capable."

She said it, and then suddenly realized it was true, and she sat a little taller.

"On a short-term basis," he replied.

"On any basis."

Giacomo sighed. "*Mi dispiace*, Gabriella. But that is my offer. I'm hesitant to stay with Baresi with the instability at the moment."

Her heart sank, but she wouldn't show it. Instead she plucked a sheaf of papers from her stack and handed it over. "You won't get the quality you want at that price, Giacomo. And if you start compromising there, your brand will weaken. Take this. Look it over. There are several options I've outlined here to, as I said, give you some flexibility and versatility. Baresi would very much like to remain your supplier. No matter if I'm sitting in the chair or if my father is."

She stood and straightened her suit jacket, then tucked her files away in her bag. Giacomo rose, too, looking a little flustered. Did he think she would stay and negotiate away all Baresi profit? If so, he had another think coming. She was stronger and smarter than that.

"Let me take you to lunch," he suggested. "We can catch up on family."

That was the last thing Gabi wanted, after attempting to establish herself as a businesswoman. "Perhaps another time, and Maria could join us?" She remembered the name of his wife—the second wife—and then added, "Or when Papa is feeling better. I know he'd enjoy seeing you both."

"I'll walk you out."

"Grazie."

She left him with a smile and a handshake—no bussing of cheeks again. And now she had a choice. She could leave and go back to Perugia right now, or she could stay in Milan for a few hours and take an afternoon off. The hotel was already booked for tonight. Why not?

It was no contest. Taking the afternoon off won.

Corsetti was located right on the edge of the Quadrilatero della Moda—Milan's fashion district. Gabi had spent hours here as a child and then a young woman, staring in the windows, admiring the fashions even though her Papa couldn't afford to shop there. Instead it was his fabrics and, in particular, cashmere that graced the elegant windows. The Baresis had a good life. A very comfortable one, but not at this level. Not at… Pemberton level.

She had her flat and there was the family villa, which was very nice, but it was certainly no château or indeed the manor house in Surrey. Still, now and again she splurged on a nice piece. Shoes, for example, or the bag she carried today, which she'd bought as a Christmas present to herself two years previous and rarely used. Today had been an appropriate occasion.

The sun was warm on her face and she slid her sunglasses over her eyes, and then ambled along the street. Via Montenapoleone was home to the biggest brands on the planet, housed in gorgeous buildings with huge arched windows and stone balustrades above. She walked past giants like Vuitton and Versace, Prada and Hermès. The store she stopped in front of was Aurora.

It wouldn't hurt to go inside, would it?

Three hours later, Gabriella had made her way out of the district and into a cab to a modest hotel. She carried a signature black-and-white bag with a splurge for herself—a soft pink cashmere sweater and a small bottle of perfume. Visiting Aurora had been fun, but it was time to get back to business.

The room was perfectly adequate, and Gabi ordered up a light meal and some wine. She set up her keyboard with her iPad and figured she might as well do some work. Her heart gave a little leap when she opened her in-box and saw an email from William.

Did you have your meeting yet? How did it go?

She wasn't sure what to say. She felt she'd stood her ground, and she thought she'd handled herself well. But she was totally unsure of the outcome.

I don't know yet. I was strong, though! He low-balled me and I told him he'll pay the price in quality if he goes elsewhere.

She waited a few minutes, read a few other emails, then his answer came back.

Good for you. Baresi has a strong product. It's why we've used you as a supplier for so long.

She laughed to herself.

That's what I said. I also gave him some options that were more cost-effective, so we'll see. I'd hate to lose a big client.

Her email was quiet for several minutes. Her dinner arrived, and she munched and sipped on the crisp wine. She had just poured a second glass when her mobile buzzed. A quick glance showed it was William.

She should ignore the little jump in her heart knowing it was him, shouldn't she?

"Hello?"

"Emailing was annoying. I thought a call might be better. Where are you?"

"In a hotel in Milan, and then starting for home early in the morning."

"You're driving?"

"It's faster than the train, even if it's not as comfortable."

"I'm glad you're not driving back tonight."

"Me, too. I drove up this morning, and ten hours of driving in one day is a lot. I'm glad I did, though. You were right about the face-to-face meeting. If nothing else, I gave him something to think about before walking away."

There was a pause, and Gabi frowned. What was William having trouble saying?

"Gabi, is…is Baresi in trouble? Seriously?"

She let out a breath. He'd seen her statements and nothing had changed. "No, not like that, Will. And I hope we don't get to that point. I just think if a client as well-known as Cor…as this one walks away, others will follow." She made the correction midsentence. There was no need to bring companies and sensitive information into it. There was trust and then there was professional discretion.

"Will you let me know if you ever get close to that point? Please?"

"I can manage, Will. I think I know what you're getting at, but no. Agreeing to that sort of proposition is what got me in trouble in the first place. Baresi will get through this."

"All right. The door is open should you need it."

"I appreciate it, but we're doing all right."

Just all right. Her worry about others following if Corsetti left was a real one. They could withstand the loss of one major client. Maybe two or three, even. More than that and the books were going to take a major hit. She put her forehead on her hand, feeling the beginning of a headache start. Maybe the best thing to do when she got back to Perugia was to hold another meeting with the sales team.

"Gabi, are you still there?"

"Yeah, I'm here." She needed to change the subject. "Do you know what I did after my meeting?"

"No, what?"

"I went into the Aurora shop. And I bought things."

"Ooh," he said. "What sorts of things?"

Some of the tension rolled off her. "A gorgeous sweater from the new fall line. And I saw the most amazing dress…a black evening gown. The attendant said that it had been designed for one of the family and then added to the fall line. Bit out of my price range."

"Ah, yes, the halter back, right? Charlotte wore that to the BAFTAs in February. It's lovely, isn't it?"

"I also bought a bottle of scent that reminds me of the garden at the château. Lavender, but also spicier notes of rosemary and thyme, and then something else…something gentler and more floral. It was like the day I sat in the garden with the sun on my face. I closed my eyes and just felt everything. The world was a million miles away."

"That's lovely."

"I would go back there if I could. Odd, but true. I felt half like a prisoner and half on vacation, but it really is the most beautiful, restful place."

"Now you can travel back when you have that scent memory," he suggested. "Maybe I need to get a bottle."

"I'm not sure it would smell the same on you," she laughed.

"No, but I could smell it and think of you," he replied, and she went quiet again.

"Will…"

"I miss you," he said bluntly.

"Will…"

"No, let me say this. I know our time together

was strange and screwed up. But what I felt…
what I feel…that's real. I don't know what to do
about it, Gabi, but to deny my feelings feels so
wrong. I wish… I wish we had time to explore
what's between us."

She did, too, but it was impossible, wasn't it?
And if she agreed with him, it would only make
it more difficult. "Maybe we should make a clean
break, Will." It killed her to say it. "This talking
and emailing makes it harder."

"Because you feel the same? Be honest."

"It won't help anything to have me say it."

He let out a huff of frustration. "It'll help me
feel like I'm not alone in this. Damn, Gabi. I feel
so alone."

Hearing him say that hurt her heart. "You have
your lovely big family," she said. She closed her
eyes and felt like crying. "But if you told them
you wanted to be with me, it would cause a total
uproar. None of them know of my agreement
with Stephen. As far as they're concerned, I
walked out on him on our wedding day. They
all think I broke his heart. Will, we've been over
this. You say you want this now, but it would
mean turning your back on your family, and they
mean everything to you. You'd end up resenting
me, and I'm not sure I can take another heart-
break."

He was quiet on the other end.

"Say something," she whispered.

"My head knows you're right. My heart doesn't want to believe you. If I told Maman the truth…"

"There's no winning here. If you told her the truth, then I haven't broken Stephen's heart but I was willing to marry him for his money. Either way I come out of this looking like the kind of woman she will not want for her son."

"Gabi, I've never felt like this before. I'm heading toward thirty and I've had girlfriends but none have made me want things I never thought I'd want."

"Why? Because I'm forbidden? A challenge?"

There was another bald silence, and she knew she'd upset him. But still, these were important questions to ask. Someone had to play devil's advocate here.

"If you really think that of me, then maybe you're right. Maybe a clean break is best."

There it was. The opportunity to walk away, do the sensible thing. It was exactly the opening she was hoping for. And instead of reaching out and grabbing it, she found herself wiping tears off her face.

"I'm sorry." She sniffed. "That was unfair of me. Oh, Will, you're the most ethical person I know. I don't think that of you. I'm just so afraid."

"Afraid of what?"

"Of…of falling for you. Of having my heart broken again. Of screwing up, just when I am starting to get myself together."

"You're falling for me?"

She choked out a laugh. "Come on, that can hardly be a surprise. Not after…" She halted as her throat closed over. That night in her flat had been so magical.

"I know," he said softly. "Gabi, I think of you all the time. I can't stop remembering what it's like to touch you. To taste you."

The air in the hotel room grew heavy. She remembered all those things, too. And then some.

"Would you consider coming to Paris for a few days?"

To what end? she wondered. What would it accomplish? And yet the idea of spending time with Will, just the two of them, sent a shaft of longing through her she couldn't deny. "I shouldn't want this so much," she whispered into the phone. "Not after such a short time. Not when it's so complicated."

"Love doesn't make sense," he replied, his voice husky. Had he used the word *love*? This was going so much faster and deeper than she knew what to do with.

"Come to Paris," his low voice persuaded. "Please. Spend a few days with me so we can sort this out face-to-face. I thought leaving you would be the end of it. I thought friends would be fine. But it's not fine, Gabi. I haven't been able to let you go."

How many women could refuse such a plea?

"Not this weekend. Next weekend. I'll fly Friday afternoon and will have to be back Sunday night."

"I'll take it. I'll take whatever time with you I can have, Gabriella."

She felt the same. And knew deep down that this weekend might be their one and only chance.

CHAPTER ELEVEN

GABI FLEW IN to Charles de Gaulle Airport early Friday evening and tried to contain the nervousness centered in her belly. She'd brought only a carry-on with her, and she shouldered the bag as she walked toward the doors leading out of the secure area. When they slid open, Will was waiting there, his eyes searching for her, and she knew.

I love him.

Then his gaze found her and connected and he smiled, and she knew a second most important thing: he loved her, too. It was on his face, in his eyes. In the connection that jolted to life the moment they laid eyes on each other. Oh, this was going to be so complicated.

"You're here." He said it when she was close enough to hear. "You're really here."

"I told you I was coming," she said, unable to contain her smile.

There was a moment where they hovered, considering a kiss. The urge to touch, to be close to him, was overwhelming, but common sense prevailed and Will stepped back. "Do you have another bag? Do we need to collect it?"

She shook her head. "No, this is it. I can pack light for two days, you know."

He laughed, the sound happy and free. "Come on, then. I have a car waiting."

Of course he did. No run-of-the-mill taxis for the Pemberton family. She found herself ensconced in black leather luxury as a driver drove away from the airport.

Will reached over for her hand. "How is your father?"

"Recovering well and getting stronger every day. The cancer hadn't spread, so that's very good news."

"I'm happy for you, and for your family. And Lucia? Giulia? Marco?"

"Mama is fussing over Papa. Giulia, I'm discovering, is very good at her job in human resources, and Marco is getting more besotted by the day. I'm not sure what's going to happen there. Giulia isn't ready to settle down."

"Is he willing to wait for her?"

"I think so. I hope so." She met Will's gaze. "I hope she's not throwing something away that is pretty incredible."

"Hmm," he said, and Gabi knew what he was thinking. They shouldn't throw away their chance, either, even if neither of them knew how to navigate the situation.

"I didn't even hug you when you arrived." Will's face took on a boyish pout and she laughed. And then he lifted his arm along the back of the seat, and she wiggled over to the middle and settled into his embrace, grateful for the tinted windows.

She closed her eyes. This was where she wanted to be. Always. Warm and loved and secure and accepted. He kissed her hair and tucked her head into his shoulder. "Oh, Gabi," he murmured. "This feels so right."

"I know."

"We're not even at my place yet, haven't even spent any time together, and yet I know what I want. I want to be with you. Really with you. Not sneaking around but a part of your life and you part of mine. I want us to own our relationship."

"I'm pretty sure my family wouldn't have a problem with that," she admitted, his words both thrilling and terrifying her. "They love you already. The day I told my parents the truth and you went upstairs? Mama asked if there was 'any hope there.' My family isn't the problem."

"I have to believe mine won't be, either, if we tell them the truth. Everyone liked you so much before."

"Yes, before I ran out on Stephen. Before they knew I was lying to them. Let's be realistic. And there's still the press to consider. Being seen together would rekindle that story."

They were quiet for a while, sitting with their own thoughts. Gabi hadn't been to Paris in a long time, but she didn't care to look out the window at the city moving past them. She kept her eyes closed and held on to Will and the fragile bond between them.

The driver dropped them at Will's apartment and Gabi tried very hard not to be overwhelmed. She had an idea what to expect—she'd been to the château and the manor, after all—but this was different. This wasn't a family space, this was Will's space, and his alone.

The first thing she noticed was the wall of windows that overlooked the river. "That is stunning." She looked at the view and then turned back. "What is it with us and views, anyway?"

"It's freedom," he replied, putting down her bag. "It's open space and possibilities and calm and a million other things that call to us. I've wanted to share this one with you ever since I got back."

And then he finally kissed her, the way she'd wanted to since first seeing him at the airport. His arms tightened around her and his mouth was sure and soft, claiming and seducing, loving and teasing. Nothing in the world was as lovely as kissing William Pemberton.

The living area before the windows was open

and furnished in soft whites and grays. It took no time at all before they were on the plush sofa, wrapped in each other's arms. "I've missed you so much," Will said. "That night in Perugia...it wasn't enough."

"I didn't want to miss you, but I did," she replied, then kissed his neck. "Oh, Will." Their lips met again, and then he pulled away and looked into her face.

"I love you, Gabriella."

It felt as if her heart expanded in her chest as the words filled her with joy, and yes, even fear. Love was such a big emotion, filled with such risk. But she couldn't stop the words from coming. "I love you, too, Will."

"We'll figure it all out. I swear we will," he promised, and somehow she believed him.

Will woke early. The sun was up but still held that thin, morning light quality to it. He slid out of bed and left Gabi sleeping on her side with her glorious hair fanned out on her pillow, the sheet tucked beneath her arms and revealing the top of her breasts. As quietly as he could, he grabbed a pair of pajama bottoms and pulled them on, tying the drawstring loosely around his hips, and then padded quietly to the kitchen. He'd start some coffee. Enjoy the quiet moments, knowing that the woman he loved was in his bed.

The water was heating and he took a few moments to quietly tidy the remnants of last night's late dinner. They'd made love first, on the rug in his living room, an urgent, hurried coming together after so many days apart. Then he'd ordered in steak frites for two, opened a bottle of wine, and they'd eaten, talking as if they'd never been apart, perhaps even freer now that they'd confessed their feelings. And then they'd made love again, slower, with a reverence that had shaken him to the core.

She didn't know, but he'd never told a woman he loved her before. At least not since he'd been seventeen, and in his mind, that really didn't count. It wasn't a love like this.

He was still trying to figure out how to bring up the matter with his family, but it was no longer a question of if but of when. He did not want this to cause a rift, but his feelings couldn't be denied, either.

But that was for later. Today he was going to enjoy every moment with Gabi that he could. She had to go home tomorrow.

He poured the first cup of coffee and had sipped away at half of it when he heard a key turn in his lock and he froze.

Charlotte, his twin sister, popped into the apartment and looked at him with surprise. "You're up! I figured I'd have to wake you. I brought breakfast. I thought we could talk about the designs for the fashion week show. I want your approval before I finalize everything."

Oh, God. Charlotte was here. Gabi was in his bedroom, wearing nothing at all. He had to get his sister out of here.

"You should have called, Charlotte." His voice held a low warning. "We didn't make plans for this. It's barely eight on a Saturday morning."

"I know, but it's coming up soon, and—"

"We can do it another time. I'll call you. It's really not a good time for me."

Her eyes widened. "You have a woman here. Oh, *mon Dieu*, I'm so sorry." Then her eyes twinkled. "Anyone I know? Is it serious?"

"Charlotte." His voice was firmer now as worry settled in his gut. "Please."

"Mmm, is that coffee I smell?"

Will froze. Gabi shuffled out of the bedroom wearing nothing but panties and one of his T-shirts. Charlotte gasped, and Gabi suddenly looked very, very awake.

"Oh," she breathed.

Charlotte's normally sweet gaze darkened. "What the hell is going on here? Will? Gabi?" She put an emphasis on Gabi's name that was more accusatory than surprise.

"I said you should have called." Will's voice was firm and none too pleased. "Now you'd better come in."

Charlotte glared at Gabi. "I can't believe this. Isn't it bad enough you jilted Stephen?"

Gabi glanced at Will, her faced tense with apology and anxiety. "I'm going to put some pants on. I'll be back." Her gaze told him she didn't expect him to handle this alone, though he was more than prepared to.

"I'll get us all some coffee," he said, and then looked at his twin. "You'd better sit down."

To his surprise, she did, but not before she dropped the bag of pastries on his counter, her lips pursed in a judgmental knot. He'd wanted to do this on his own time, when they were ready, when they'd figured out exactly how they wanted to handle his family. For heaven's sake, they'd only just said I love you to each other.

He hadn't been ready to fall in love. He certainly wasn't ready to deal with the family fallout.

He poured coffee, fixed Charlotte's and Gabi's the way he knew they liked, and as he took the mugs to the dining table, Gabi came out of the bedroom dressed in yoga pants and still in his T-shirt. He liked that she hadn't changed. In some way, keeping his shirt on seemed like maintaining ownership of their relationship. Not hiding away, when it would be so easy to.

He sat down with his own mug, looked Charlotte in the eye and said, "Yes. Gabi and I are together. We weren't going to tell anyone yet because it's new to us, too. But I'm not going to lie to you, Charlotte, and pretend this is something it's not."

Charlotte looked at Gabi and scowled. "So you left one brother for another. Nice."

Gabi curled her hands around her mug and met Charlotte's gaze. "I never should have agreed to marry Stephen. We were never in love, Charlotte. We made a big mistake, getting engaged."

"How convenient for you."

Gabi laughed a little. "Trust me, this is anything but convenient." Then she looked at Will. "Your brother was sent in to do damage control and…it just happened. Despite both of us saying it couldn't and shouldn't." She smiled a little, and Will reached over and put his hand over hers.

"Oh, yuck." Charlotte was not convinced. "And you, doing this to your own brother. I'm disgusted with you."

"It isn't what it seems, Charlotte."

"What does that mean?"

"It means you should ask Stephen about his relationship with Gabi. I love my brother. God, you know I do." He held her gaze and knew she understood. She knew what Stephen had done for him. "You know I would never hurt him. But what am I supposed to do, throw away the best thing that's ever happened to me because it's messy?"

"Will." Gabi's voice was soft and full of

amazement, and he tore his eyes from Charlotte and looked at her instead.

"It's true," he admitted. "I've never felt this way about anyone."

"Me, either."

Charlotte made a sound of disgust and stood. "Ugh, I can't do this. Gabriella, I liked you when Stephen brought you home. But since then you've left him at the altar, caused a PR disaster, apparently seduced my other brother, and now you're both creating another scandal. I don't understand you."

"I know it looks that way," Gabi replied, "but you've only got part of the story. It's not my place to reveal Stephen's secrets. And you're quite right that I'm not innocent in all this. Let me just say that not marrying Stephen was my attempt to make things right, not cause trouble. And falling for Will was pure accident."

"That makes no sense at all."

"I know, and I'm sorry. The truth is, Will and I haven't had a chance to figure out how we wanted to tell your family. So I'm saying less than I might otherwise, out of respect for both your brothers."

Charlotte stared at Will, and looked angrier than he could ever remember. "If you think I'm keeping your dirty little secret, you're sadly mistaken."

"I don't expect you to. Hoped you might, but don't expect it."

"Don't try to guilt me, Will."

"I'm not."

"And you." She stared at Gabi. "If you think this is another way to get your hands on Pemberton money, forget it. Maman will never allow it."

"That's enough, Charlotte." Will stood now. Anger he understood. Of course Charlotte wouldn't understand, especially when appearances were so damning. But he also wouldn't stand for Gabi being abused.

"It's okay, Will. It's no more than I expected."

Charlotte grabbed her handbag and headed for the door. "I've heard enough. If you can dig your head out of your little love nest long enough, I'd like a meeting early this week. In my office."

"I appreciate the summons."

With one last scathing look, his sister slammed out the door.

He looked down at Gabi, who was sitting looking a bit shell-shocked. "I'm so sorry. She let herself in with her key and you came out before I could get her to leave."

"It was bound to happen sometime. And like I said, I expected it. And more. Stephen will lose his mind and I'm sure your mother will be equally angry."

"Arabella might be okay. She's more the type who listens to all sides and makes up her own mind. Not that it won't be weighted against us. I know that. But Bella is reasonable. And Christophe…he tries to please everyone. He'll stay quiet and out of the drama."

Will knew his cousin had never quite felt like a brother, even though he'd been practically raised by Aurora and Cedric. Mostly he tried to not make any extra waves, which Will thought was a shame. His cousin was smart and far more savvy than most gave him credit for.

Gabi slumped in her chair and took a drink of cooling coffee. "So what do we do now?"

"I don't know. Let's sit tight for a while and see what happens. For once, getting ahead of the story might not do us any favors. Charlotte is probably already on the phone with Stephen. Let's see how this all plays out before we make a plan to change minds."

She put down her cup and looked at him sadly. "It is worth it, right?" she asked, her voice wobbling. "I do love you, you know."

"It's worth it," he confirmed, sitting next to her again.

"I won't let you have to make a choice."

His heart warmed. "Oh, darling, I know that. If anyone forces a choice, it'll be my family. And that makes me sad. But it can't stop me from loving you. I never had a choice in that."

Still, the atmosphere in the apartment had turned to one of sadness and worry. Will had made all sorts of romantic plans for the day, but pushed them aside. What they needed now was to stick together. And so they went back into the bedroom, crawled under the covers and held on to each other while they waited for the storm to break.

CHAPTER TWELVE

IT DIDN'T TAKE LONG.

First Bella called, asking if Will was sure about what he was doing, at least attempting to be fair as she agreed that there seemed to be more to the story than a runaway bride and the groom's brother. Will hung up not quite sure he had an ally, but at least one person who was willing to listen.

The next phone call came early in the afternoon, and was from his mother. It didn't go as well as the call with Bella. It became clear to Will that Stephen had not enlightened anyone as to the original agreement between himself and Gabi. It was very difficult to hear Gabi spoken about in unfavorable terms, and to have his own family loyalty questioned. Gabi was right about one thing. The truth about the fake marriage would end up making her look like a gold digger.

Gabi was unusually quiet, her face pensive. Their romantic weekend was a disaster. Would their entire relationship be this way? Could they handle it, especially living so far apart? Will listened to his mother's voice in his ear and closed his eyes, pinching the bridge of his nose. He and Gabi were supposed to work this out gradually. Tell people when they were ready, when they had a handle on their relationship. Will, who prided himself on his ability to clean up messes, now found himself in the middle of the biggest one yet, and no clue how to fix it, other than let Gabi go.

He pondered it for exactly two seconds, before his stubborn nature rose up and rebelled. If he buckled under the pressure now, he'd regret it forever. He was not the same boy who'd been rash and impulsive and seeking attention. He was a grown man who'd worked very hard to become who he was. He wouldn't let anyone put him back in that box.

"Maman, what I'm saying is you need to talk to Stephen. Can you do that and then we can talk again?"

He listened to her for another moment, then replied, "Because it is his story to tell, not mine." William had never been, and never would, be a tattletale, even now that they were grown men.

The call ended and he sighed deeply.

"I'm so sorry, Will. I should go home. This is causing nothing but strife."

"I can handle it, but I understand if you want to go home. This is not the weekend I promised."

Instead of getting out of the bed, she slid closer and wrapped her arms around his middle. "It was going to happen eventually. We just thought we had more time."

"It's a lot of pressure on a new relationship."

She nodded against his chest. "Yes, but we're not exactly conventional."

He chuckled at that. How did she have the ability to make him laugh in the midst of such a horrible day?

His phone buzzed and he looked down. It was a text this time, not a call, but it hurt his heart more than any conversation he'd had thus far today.

So much for loyalty.

He put the phone aside, regret weighing heavily.

"From Stephen?"

He nodded.

"I'm sorry. Maybe this is a mistake, Will. It isn't fair to put you through this. I'd rather walk away than see you lose your family. I can't imagine if this were my papa and mama and Giulia."

He thought back to the day she'd confessed the "plan" to her parents at the villa. There had been instant forgiveness and acceptance. Why did his family not trust him the same way? He understood they were trying to protect him, but why could they not give him the benefit of the doubt?

Was it because despite all the hard work of the last four years, he was still the screw up who'd fought an addiction and nearly tossed his life away?

For the briefest of moments he let those feelings in. Feelings of being a disappointment and a failure. Feelings of being a burden. And then he sniffed, sat up a little taller. He'd changed, grown, and had worked so hard to make up for the worry he'd caused. That was the man his family needed to see. Not the troubled boy.

"Will?"

He turned to her. "Stay. Forget about my family for twenty-four hours and stay with me. Love me. They can wait. We get to decide what we want, so let's do that."

"If you're sure…"

"I'm sure." In fact, he'd never been surer of anything. "Let's get out of here, get a hotel and hide away."

"That sounds a lot like running away."

He shook his head. "No, darling. It's a tactical retreat. Sometimes you concede the battle to win the war, and we're going to win them over, you'll see."

* * *

Gabi sighed, tucked her hair behind her ears and, for the first time in her adult life, considered day drinking.

Corsetti had not renewed their contract. When word got out, two smaller clients pulled their agreements as well. Massimo was home after his second round of chemotherapy and going through the full gamut of side effects. Her job was to save the company, not chase all their clients away.

And she didn't even have Will here for moral support. He'd visited the weekend before last, spending two days at the villa with her and her parents. He hadn't minded sleeping in his own room, he'd assured her. So they'd kept to separate rooms, but swam in the pool and walked the grounds and spent time together free of criticism or pressure.

Basically she'd spent forty-eight hours in denial about the mess of her life.

She looked at the financial projections again and sighed, then called the head of sales and set up a meeting for the following Tuesday. Tomorrow would have been preferable, but this time she was flying to London. Will was meeting her there and they were going to Chatsworth Hall together, for Aurora's birthday.

Gabi was so nervous about it she'd barely eaten in three days and was constantly nauseated. It was her first time back at Chatsworth, first time seeing the family again, and it was the matriarch's fifty-sixth birthday. No pressure at all.

At the end of the workday, she made her way home to her flat and packed her bag for the weekend. She would have to dress smartly, even when she wasn't at the party. She had her favorite standby little black dress for that occasion, and fine heels that would put her closer to Will's lovely height.

And then she sat on her bed and wondered if she could get on the plane, after all. If she was strong enough.

Her phone dinged twice, indicating a text message. She lifted it and laughed. How could he know? One short sentence was all it took to give her a smidge of courage.

Don't even think about canceling.

She typed back.

How did you know?

The reply came across the screen and she laughed when she saw it.

LOL. I would.

But she wouldn't. For all her insecurities, she trusted that Will wanted to be with her. He was the master at making things right, wasn't he? And so he would again, somehow. If he was brave enough to stand up to his family, she would match his courage by being by his side.

The last time Gabi had flown into Heathrow, she'd taken the Express into the station and then cabbed it to Stephen's house in St. John's Wood. This time, however, she flew into Gatwick and Will met her there. They made the drive to Chatsworth Hall in Will's car, a peppy little thing that made her wonder how he could ever fit behind the wheel with his long legs. It was drizzling, and the drive was not as picturesque as she remembered. The traffic on the A281 was heavy and Gabi's nerves made her muscles tense. She wasn't sure how she could make it through a whole weekend like this.

"It's going to be okay," Will promised. "The family will come around."

"You're optimistic," she said darkly, but he reached over and took her hand. "They need to know the truth, that's all."

Gabi knew he thought that, but she'd had a different thought. They didn't just need to know the truth, they needed to believe it. And in the weeks since Charlotte had walked in on them in

Will's flat, Stephen had not once offered any additional information.

"So what's the plan for tonight?"

"A quiet dinner on our own. Tomorrow is Maman's party. Just family, but she's planning a lavish meal and it's cocktail dress."

"I brought something suitable." She was at least confident in her dress and appearance. That was the only thing she was confident about.

"If you like, we can go out riding tomorrow. Or into Bramley to browse around."

"Let's not make anything firm. Being locked into plans makes me even more nervous."

"Sweetheart. We're in this together."

They drove on for several minutes before Gabi spoke up again. "Do you ever wonder if we're being crazy? Falling so hard, so fast?" Her heart hammered in her chest. "What if they're right, Will? What if we're being foolish?"

He glanced over, his lips thin, though he kept his voice carefully even. "Do you think we're being foolish?"

"Maybe." Her stomach somersaulted as she said it.

"Do you think what we have is real?"

She blinked against sudden tears. "I'm sure it is. I've never felt this way. Not even with Luca."

"Then relax. The course of true love never did run smooth."

She reached over and gave his arm a little

punch, but she smiled a bit. It was three days. Not even three whole days. If they could get through this, they could get through anything and it would be smooth sailing.

The lane to the manor finally appeared and Gabi felt a bit of déjà vu as they drove up to the house. She'd come here only weeks ago, and while she had changed, the house and the gardens had not. Oh, perhaps a few blooms had gone out of season and others had taken their place, but everything else was as majestic and perfect as she remembered.

"Home sweet home," Will murmured, and despite his light words, she saw his jaw was set.

He stopped the car and killed the engine, then reached over and took her hand as he looked in her eyes in one last private moment before going inside. "Together," he said firmly. "We do this together."

"Together," she echoed, though she thought she sounded far more confident than she felt.

The only one at home was Arabella, and they encountered her only five minutes after entering. She was coming down the stairs just as they were preparing to go up, and halted on a small landing where the stairs made a turn.

"Bella," Will said, his voice unsure.

Bella looked from Will to Gabi, and back to Will again. "You have guts, I'll give you that," she said, but then she smiled and gracefully descended several more steps to meet them. She held her hand out to Gabi. "Gabriella," she said quietly. "Welcome back to the lion's den."

Gabi gasped and laughed at the same time, and Bella's eyes twinkled a bit. Gabi understood that while she was on notice, this woman could be a potential ally, and that wasn't something she took lightly. "Thank you, Bella."

"Stephen is in London and coming down tomorrow. Christophe will be here late tonight, and Charlotte and Maman are flying in together from Paris in the morning." The itinerary gave Gabi an idea of what to expect when, and from whom. "Tonight it's just us. You can breathe a bit easier. I'm trying to keep an open mind and be Switzerland."

"Thank you, Bella. That means a lot."

She pinned Gabi with an assessing look. "I do expect some sort of an explanation, though. With this sort of family drama, it's hard to go on faith, you understand."

Gabi nodded quickly. "I do, and of course."

Will squeezed her hand reassuringly. "We'll scare up some food in the kitchen in a bit. But maybe a glass of wine later?"

"That sounds perfect. You go get settled. It's going to be a bumpy ride."

As Bella continued down the stairs, Gabi and Will continued up, Will carrying their bags.

"You're staying in my room," he decreed. "I'm not leaving you alone for any sneak attacks."

Gabi tried to keep a sense of humor as he led her down a long, carpeted hall. "Hmm. So you've gone from my jailer to my protector. Interesting."

"Isn't it just?" He opened a door on the left and drew her inside, then closed it and pinned her against the solid wood, kissing her so thoroughly she was quite breathless. "I've been wanting to do that for an hour and a half," he growled, and then feasted again on her willing mouth.

"Okay," she said when they finally came up for air. "We've established that we're still wildly attracted to each other. It's a good start."

He laughed and gathered her into his arms for a massive hug. "You are a joy," he murmured in her ear. "And a gift. I'd be a fool to let that go. Remember that when things get tense, okay? Joy. Fool."

She nodded against his chest and wrapped her arms around him. It would be okay. Will wouldn't let anything bad happen.

Gabi took some time to unpack, though it only took a few minutes as she'd packed lightly for the weekend. Will had arrived that morning, and his things were already tucked away. Including a tux for the following night, she noticed. "A tuxedo?"

"For birthday celebrations? Always." He grinned. "Have you seen me in a tuxedo? I'm really quite dashing."

She met his gaze and frowned. "The day of the wedding, remember?"

He slapped his head. "How could I have forgotten?"

They were still chuckling about it when they made their way down to the kitchens and Will fixed them thick sandwiches with sour pickles and then jam tarts that their cook had made that morning. As they ate, they caught up on more "normal" things, like work and her father's health.

"You've had a rough go with your client list lately. Have you told your father?"

She frowned, her brow wrinkling. "No, not yet. When he's had his treatment and feels awful, it seems wrong to add to it. And when he's perked up before his next treatment, it seems unfair to ruin it by giving him bad news."

Will bit down on his pickle. "You should, though. He'd want to know what was happening."

"I know. I'll find a way to tell him when I get back."

"He might welcome a chance to be part of the business, you know. Feel useful and connected."

"You mean, instead of not worrying, he might be worrying about what he doesn't know?"

Will shrugged. "Maybe. How many have you lost?"

"Three big accounts, a few smaller ones.

Baresi was already feeling a pinch. I'm worried, Will."

"Any new accounts? How's your sales department doing?"

"We've picked up a few new ones, but certainly not enough to make up for the losses."

He nodded sagely, and seemed lost in thought for a few minutes. "What are you thinking?" she asked.

"Just pondering solutions. I'll let you know if I come up with anything."

"Thanks."

They tidied up together, and then went to the drawing room. Will wandered through and then stopped at a small table set up with a chessboard. "My father used to play with anyone who would take him on," he said, warm reminiscence in his voice. "Do you know how?"

"I haven't for years, but yes." She went to the table and pulled out a chair, settling in. "You'll beat me, but I can take it."

"I never beat Papa. Not once."

"It wouldn't be right to trounce the earl."

"No, it damned well wouldn't."

They played for a while. Gabi held her own, but Will was more strategic and she was losing ground when Arabella entered, still dressed in her casual pants and the soft green sweater that skimmed her arms to the wrist. "I brought a good, full cabernet from the cellar," she said, holding a bottle aloft. "Anyone interested?"

"I will, because your brother is about to beat me soundly. Now we can call it a draw."

"Not if you concede."

"Hah," she answered, but grinned at him.

Bella went to a side table and uncorked the wine, then decanted it. "You really do care about each other, don't you?"

"What makes you say that?" Will moved to get three glasses.

"How you talk to each other. How you look at each other. It's the real deal."

Gabi put her hand on Bella's arm. "That's the nicest thing you possibly might have said, and I appreciate it."

"Oh, you still have some explaining to do." Bella started to pour wine in the glasses. "But at least I believe that you care for each other. Either that or you're a hell of an actress, Gabi. I mean, we all thought you loved Stephen." She looked Gabi over with an eagle eye. "But you look at Will differently."

The three of them settled down together. Gabi took a sip—it was truly excellent—and then took a breath. "Will, I think I should be the one to tell her the truth. After all, I'm the one who ran. I'm the one no one trusts."

"If you're sure."

Gabi looked at Bella. "You've been fair so far.

If I have to do this again tomorrow, I'd like to at least make a first run at it with someone who is open to listening."

Bella lifted her glass in a small toast. "Go on, then."

Gabi took a drink of wine and then laid out the entire timeline, right up until the morning of the wedding. As she got to the part about Will showing up at the hotel, he interrupted. "I told her that her timing left a lot to be desired, but not the decision. It was a crazy plan and I never liked it."

"You knew?" Bella's lips dropped open.

"I knew. About Bridget, about his plans for Gabi." He leaned forward. "Why else do you think I was the one to go clean up the mess?"

Bella sat back on the sofa and sighed. She met Gabi's gaze. "So you're double damned. If the family doesn't know the truth, you've jilted Stephen at the altar. If they do, then you were marrying him for the money. You don't come out looking good, no matter what."

"Just so." This time Gabi lifted her glass in a mock salute.

"Except you don't have Stephen or the money," Bella pointed out.

"No, but I've moved on to his brother. Charlotte pointed that out."

Bella nodded. "Except this time it's real."

Gabi turned her head and looked at Will. He

was watching her with such adoration she melted. "Oh, yes," she agreed. "It's so very real."

Bella got up and grabbed the wine bottle, then topped up the glasses. "Will, you are the most honorable man I know. I believe you," she said firmly. "But, so help me God, if I'm wrong, I'm going to strangle you both. And then throw you to Maman."

CHAPTER THIRTEEN

THE BIRTHDAY PARTY of Aurora Germain Pemberton was small but a sparkling affair. She would never have it any other way, and William gave one final tug on his bow tie before turning to look at Gabi, who was nervously twisting her fingers as she waited for him.

William wanted to tell her to relax, but he knew it was an impossible request. Tonight she truly was walking into the lion's den, as Bella had put it. The entire family was here: Aurora, of course, and Bella, Stephen, Christophe and his current girlfriend, Lizzy, Charlotte and of course Will and Gabi. Will hoped that the presence of Lizzy meant everyone would be on their best behavior, but there was no guarantee of that.

Gabi looked stunning, though. The little black dress skimmed her curves beautifully, and her black heels were simple but he recognized the quality. He'd come to notice something about Gabi. She did not have an endless wardrobe but what she chose was high quality and classic.

Since those were the basic principles behind his mother's fashion dynasty, there was nothing to fault in her appearance.

"You are so beautiful," he murmured, holding out his hand. "I'm the luckiest man in England."

She laughed a little. "You're foolish, but I appreciate the compliment."

"It's going to be fine," he said, more confidently than he felt. But one thing he was sure of: he would stand beside her. She hadn't cowered; she'd come to face them all, and at the scene of the crime. That took a lot of strength.

They made their way down to the drawing room for before-dinner drinks. Gabi clutched his hand so tightly his fingers hurt, but he wouldn't say a word about it. She was entitled. When they walked in, a hush fell over the room as several pairs of eyes landed on them.

And then the conversation sparked up again as they were…ignored.

"Let's get a drink," Will suggested.

"Just soda or tonic or something for me," Gabi whispered. "I think I'll go light on the alcohol tonight."

"Fair." He kept his voice low. He headed to the bar and poured himself a gin and tonic and added a fresh wedge of lime. Bella appeared at their side and smiled, though her eyes were troubled. "Here we go," she said. "Gabi, would you like a drink?" She said it loudly enough that others might hear her being at least polite. Will appreciated her trying to set the tone.

"Maybe a white wine spritzer?"

"Good choice. I'll get it." Bella adeptly poured some wine in a glass and added club soda. "Lime?"

"No, thank you." She accepted the glass. "Thank you, Bella," she whispered.

"Don't thank me yet."

Will and Gabi held their drinks but it soon became clear that the family strategy was to pretend they didn't exist. Will took Gabi's hand and led her to his mother, whom he wished happy birthday. She kissed his cheek but her eyes only glanced over Gabi and she said nothing to her. The snub was brutally obvious, though subtle.

Charlotte looked their way and then turned her back, talking to Stephen, who stood with his hand in his suit pocket, being ever the earl, commanding the room almost as much as their mother.

Resentment burned in Will's veins. They weren't even making an effort. He wanted to call them out on it, but he wouldn't give them the satisfaction. He would not ruin the party or make things more difficult for Gabi. He would choose his moment.

Christophe finally took pity on them and approached with Lizzy, a model from London who, while no stranger to celebrity, seemed very shy and lovely. Will sent Christophe a look of gratitude, which his cousin acknowledged with a slight nod. Lizzy was the perfect buffer, at least for now. She and Gabi chatted easily.

They went into dinner and Gabi and her ally were separated, being seated at different sides of the table. Will noticed that Gabi picked at her food but really didn't eat much from each course. The conversation was never directed their way, and William's anger multiplied. He was still a part of this family. He put his hand on Gabi's thigh under the table, a small gesture of togetherness. She put her hand over his and squeezed, then looked at him and smiled weakly.

She was here and she was trying. And Will's anger continued to bubble.

After several courses that Will couldn't remember tasting, the cake was brought in, a beautiful white cream cake with fresh fruit. Corks popped as champagne was opened to accompany the cake, and it was sliced and served beautifully on the Pemberton china.

If his father were here, he wouldn't have stood for this. Will knew it deep in his soul. Cedric Pemberton had been a fair man, always willing to listen, to give people a chance even when others were against them. Look at Maman. She came from humble beginnings and had married an earl, and if Will remembered correctly, his grandparents hadn't been overly fond of the idea, either.

He was just about to say as much when Gabi

touched his elbow. "Will you excuse me for a moment, Will? I need to go to the powder room."

"Of course." He smiled into her eyes. "Are you coming back?"

She lifted an eyebrow. "I'm not running away, if that's what you're asking."

"That's my girl," he replied. "I'll be here."

She slipped out of the dining room while the rest of the family rose from the table and circulated with their champagne. The formal part of dinner was over. If they could get through the next thirty minutes or so of mingling, they were in the clear.

Gabi locked the powder room door and let out a breath as her chin dropped. It had been a good ninety minutes of constant tension and being under a microscope. Bella had been polite, and Christophe's girlfriend was a godsend, but she hadn't been able to completely ignore the stand-offishness of Stephen, Charlotte and Aurora. It was like she didn't exist.

Five minutes. She just needed five minutes of peace to regroup and then she could face the rest of the evening. She sat on the closed toilet lid and closed her eyes, then took several long, slow breaths.

When she felt she was ready again, she opened the door, only to find Stephen leaning against the wall on the opposite side of the hall.

"Oh," she said, immediately wary and confused.

"I wanted a chance to talk to you alone. I wasn't sure William would let me, he's so protective. Though I can understand that, considering his motives."

She frowned. "Motives? You mean not leaving me to the wolves? You said what you needed to say at the villa, Stephen." She started to walk away, but Stephen's voice called her back.

"He's using you."

She turned back, angry that he would try to drive a wedge between them. "William has been nothing but wonderful, even while his family has shunned him because of it."

"He doesn't want you. Why do you think I turned down his plan? At least I was honest about what I wanted out of our...alliance. Will is making you think he's in love with you, when what he wants is control of Baresi." He stepped away from the wall. "I said no to the acquisition to protect you, not punish you."

Gabi stared at him. It wasn't true. She didn't believe him. "This is sour grapes, and so beneath you, Stephen. We were friends once."

His gaze sharpened. "Yes, we were."

Nausea rolled in her stomach again, and it had little to do with the rich sauce she'd eaten earlier. It was the tiniest bit of doubt. "You're wrong."

But in the back of her mind she was thinking about all the things she'd told Will. He'd been

supportive in his comments but hadn't really offered firm advice. She'd told him about clients
they'd lost, their financial situation, how new
clients were hard to come by…all the information he'd need if he wanted to move in and make
an offer.

No. She would not believe it of Will.

But then, she'd believed a lot of things. She'd
believed Luca wanted to marry her and have a
family. She'd believed in Stephen, too, and while
his words were causing her great concern, she
realized she didn't trust him. What if he was
right about Will? Her father had put Baresi in
her hands. He'd trusted her with everything. Had
she misplaced her trust by trusting William? And
then she thought back to all the times when her
gut had said she maybe shouldn't trust Will, and
she wondered if she might be sick. What if her
intuition had been right?

"Be careful, Gabi."

"I don't believe you. You haven't even told
your own family the truth of our engagement."

He stepped forward then, holding her gaze.
"You know I don't let people into my intimate
business."

"You're letting them think I'm with Will for
his money."

"You're really in love with him. God, he's
played this perfectly."

Her heart took the hit. She didn't want to believe it, but she'd been played before. She would be a fool to not consider the possibility now. Not with so much at stake.

She should have been talking to her father about the business, not Will. Fear clogged her throat.

"Please think about it, Gabriella."

He walked away then, as nonchalantly as ever, in his perfectly tailored tuxedo. She had trusted him and he had done nothing to break that trust, really. She had been the one to run from their wedding. At the villa he'd been angry and hurt and humiliated. And rude, but...to her knowledge, he'd never outright lied.

Stephen was gone when Will came around the corner, his face wreathed in concern. "Are you all right? You've been gone a long time."

She wanted to cry. She loved him, she did. She didn't want to believe what Stephen had said, but he'd planted the damned seed and she couldn't help herself. "I'm not feeling very well, it turns out," she replied. "I was going to find you and make my excuses. I think dinner was a little too rich."

"Are you sick?"

She bit down on her lip. "Close."

"Of course. We can leave the party now."

"Not both of us. Just me, William. You should stay. It's your mother's birthday."

"Then I'll follow shortly, after saying my

goodbyes." He leaned forward and kissed her cheek. "You're cold," he murmured.

"I'm fine. I just need to lie down."

"I'll be right along, I promise." The concern on his face scored her heart. Why, why had Stephen made her doubt even the smallest bit?

He squeezed her hand before turning away. "Go put on something cozy and rest," he advised. Then he met her gaze again. "I love you, Gabi."

If he didn't go right now she was going to burst into tears. "I love you, too," she answered, knowing it was true, wondering if it was wrong.

He smiled, and she memorized every feature of his handsome face. He couldn't be guilty of what Stephen said. He couldn't. Will strode back toward the dining room, and she stumbled toward the stairs, fighting tears. The moments they'd shared, making love, the soul-to-soul connection…it had to be real.

She opened the bedroom door and then rushed to the bathroom and was sick. Not from the food, but from the stress and the possibility that she had once again made a bad decision. She'd believed that she and Luca had had that connection, too, and he'd been a liar and a fraud and a cheat.

What she needed now was time and space. To think. To decide what to do now. She washed her face and put on the nightgown she'd brought, one that was much too sexy for the situation but she'd brought nothing else to sleep in. She was sitting in bed, with earbuds in her ears, when Will came in.

She pulled out the earbuds.

"What are you listening to?"

"A meditation."

He instantly went to the bed and sat on the edge. "I'm so sorry about how my family reacted." He smiled. "I'm used to their dramatics. I promise it'll pass eventually, when they see we're committed."

"I'm not sure of that," she replied, looking down.

"They will. Bella is already halfway there and I can always count on Christophe." He put a finger under her chin and lifted it, tried a winning smile, but she didn't have it in her to give one in return. "Sweetheart, what is it? Is it my family, or your family situation? You've been under so much stress. Damn that Stephen. If he had only agreed to my proposal, so much of this burden would have been lessened for you."

Her stomach clenched. "It isn't for you to save Baresi. I can do this on my own."

"I've been giving it more thought the last few weeks," he said, sliding further onto the bed so they were face-to-face. "We don't need Aurora to officially invest. I have my own money. I can help you."

The proposition struck her speechless for several seconds. Had he mentioned this to his brother? That he was planning to go off book and make an offer himself?

"No, William." She slid out of the bed and went to the closet to take out her robe. She slid it over her shoulders and tied the belt firmly. "I don't want your money. I'm going to deal with this on my own."

"But, darling, it could make things so much easier for you. Like we planned at the villa, remember?"

She remembered, and she'd felt desperate at the time, with her father's surgery still looming and so much uncertainty. Now, even though she was struggling in her new position, she wasn't nearly as afraid of it. Not so much that she was willing to cede control to anyone. Not even Will.

"Maybe I don't need easy. Maybe I need to accomplish this myself. And I certainly don't need you coming in and taking over."

He stood and stared at her. "Taking over? Who said anything about taking over?"

"It would be a great addition to your own business interests, wouldn't it? And then you could be the one to negotiate with Aurora and you'd be padding your pockets from both sides." She shook her head. "I can't believe I didn't see it before."

His mouth dropped open. "I can't believe you just said that. Gabi."

"Maybe I've been gullible this whole time.

What a perfect mark I was, trying to avoid a scandal, vulnerable because of my father...you could swoop in as my rescuer and achieve what Stephen could not."

He swore quite thoroughly. "Who the hell got to you? What did they say? This is ridiculous!"

"Is it?" Fear and desperation nudged her forward. "You always said that loyalty to your family comes first, particularly to Stephen." She thought back to that day at the villa when Stephen and Will had fought. "What happened between you at my house?" she asked. "Did Stephen not like your plan?"

Will ran his hand through his hair, clearly frustrated. "This is unbelievable. An hour ago we were united against the world. And now you're accusing me of using you to take over your company? Someone must have said something to you. What I don't understand is why you'd believe them."

Gabi heard hurt in his voice and didn't know what to believe. He hadn't actually denied it, but he hadn't confirmed it, either. And Stephen had been convincing, playing the friend card. She shook her head. "Do you know what? I don't trust any of you right now. I don't know who to believe."

"So someone did get to you."

"It doesn't mean they were lying."

He stared at her, and the longer he did, the

more confused she became. Why couldn't she trust him? Why couldn't she believe him? And then she remembered telling Luca she might be pregnant and the look of horror on his face as he crushed her future beneath his heel. She remembered the horrible sick feeling as she waited for the pregnancy test results, and the combined sadness and relief she felt. She remembered the panic of her wedding day, and dashing off in Stephen's car to hide away in London, knowing she'd been foolish to agree to his plan in the first place.

The truth was, she had a history of making bad decisions, and there was too much at stake to do it again.

"I don't trust my own judgment," she said, her voice as even as she could make it. "I don't know who or what to believe. And if that's the case, I think... I think I need some time and distance away to think things through."

"You're giving up on us."

"I'm choosing what I know is real. I need to go home. And I need to sort through my life. This was all such a mistake."

And yet her heart cracked as she said it. The pain nearly stole her breath. Her heart was screaming for her to trust him and remember all the ways he'd been there for her. Her head was challenging her to think about his motives.

"Please, don't do anything rash. We can talk

about this tomorrow. Think about what you're saying, and don't let fear or my family's meanness drive you away. Please, Gabi. This is too important to throw away."

"I think I need to sleep alone tonight, Will. I have a lot to sort through."

He hesitated, and she hoped he wouldn't insist. The idea of lying beside him in the bed, trying to hold her emotions in check, was overwhelming. She needed to cry, and then to really sort things out.

"I'll go to another room," he acquiesced, though he sounded upset about it. "If that's what you need."

"I do."

"And we'll sort this out in the morning."

She nodded.

He paused, and she wondered if he was going to try and kiss her or hug her before leaving the room. In the end he sent her a complicated look of love and fear and left, shutting the door quietly behind him.

She went back to the bed and sat on the edge, expecting to cry. Instead her eyes remained dry as she sat for long minutes. For the first time ever, her emotions were too big for tears.

She needed to go home.

CHAPTER FOURTEEN

WILL WOKE AND went to the room where Gabi slept. He knocked on the door, but there was no answer. And he knew what he would find before he finished opening the door.

She was gone.

A helplessness overwhelmed him as he stared at the room. The bed was perfectly made, as if no one had been there at all. And on the night table was a folded note. God, just like last time. For a second he felt played and understood how Stephen must have felt that day at the chapel. Except Stephen hadn't loved her. Will did.

He picked it up carefully, as if it might bite, and unfolded the thick cream paper. *Dear Will*, it began, and there were several lines beneath the salutation.

At least it was better than Stephen's brief *Please forgive me.*

Dear Will,
I know you're going to be furious that I've

run again, but I have to go home. I have to
sort out what is real and what isn't in my
head. I do not know who to trust. Maybe
I've been manipulated too many times, or
maybe I'm a horrible judge of people. I just
don't trust myself to make the right decision.

I'm afraid, Will. Afraid that I'll do the
wrong thing and in doing so ruin everything.

I want to believe everything between us
was real, but I can't. That doubt is there,
and I can't shake it. And that is no way to
have a relationship. I'm sorry.
Gabi

He folded the page into quarters and tucked
it into his pocket. She hadn't doubted him until
last night when she'd excused herself, so what
had happened in that fifteen minutes? He tried to
think of who might have spoken to her, but they
were all mingling and enjoying cake and champagne at the time. He'd been talking to Christophe, and couldn't account for everyone else at
the time.

But someone had, and he was going to find
out who.

Within three minutes he'd banged on everyone's door and announced a family meeting immediately in the library. This was going to end
now. No more secrets. No more maneuvering.
And no more putting up with sneaky behavior

in the name of loyalty. It had to work both ways, and he was owed some, too.

It took half an hour for everyone to congregate. Bella was cool as ever, in jeans and a sweater, her hair up in a topknot. Christophe's hair, on the other hand, was smushed on one side and he had a good bit of stubble on his chin. Lizzy was still in bed, he said, and out of the family drama. Charlotte looked supremely annoyed and attended in her silk pajamas and robe, and Aurora, as ever, was fully dressed, hair perfect, and her "day" makeup on.

"No coffee?" Charlotte complained, and Will silenced her with a look.

He took the note out of his pocket and held it up. "If someone helped Gabi catch a ride to the airport, I'd like to know right now."

No one said a word, but Aurora lifted one eyebrow and Stephen looked slightly smug.

"You're probably amused that I, too, got a runaway note," Will said, glaring at Stephen. "But I'm going to say this. Gabi has been manipulated, and not by me. One of you spoke to her last night and portrayed our relationship as one of opportunity and not love. And I'm here to say that whoever did that has betrayed me in the biggest way because I love her. I love her and she loves me and someone has made her doubt that."

No one spoke.

"Charlotte? You've been against this since you found out in Paris. Was it you?"

"No." She nodded at the note. "But I'd say that note is evidence that whoever did, did you a favor."

He was so angry. So very, very angry and afraid. What if he couldn't figure out a way to get her back?

William looked at his mother. There was something in her eyes he didn't expect. Compassion. He knew it wasn't her. She might not approve, but she wouldn't actively poison the well. She knew what it was like to be distrusted and disliked by a man's family. And so that left...

Stephen.

"You're my brother. I can't believe you'd be this malicious."

Stephen met Will's gaze. "It was business."

"Like hell it was."

"Face it, Will. Your proposal would have put you in a fine position to take control of Baresi. I just said that I couldn't let that happen."

"Stephen." That was from Aurora, a stern admonishment. "Will would never do that."

"No, I wouldn't." If they weren't in his father's library, and if his mother weren't here, he'd be tempted to take Stephen down a notch or two.

"But see? She doesn't trust you. You're better off," Stephen said. "I'm just looking out for you, little brother."

"No, you're not." Bella stepped in this time. "Stephen, I know about your stupid agreement with Gabi. If you start with the 'left at the altar broken heart' thing, *I'm* going to knock you into next week."

Three sets of eyes looked from Bella to Stephen.

"Are you going to tell them or shall I?" Will asked.

"Tell us what?" Aurora's voice was soft but imperious, a tone they'd all learned to take very seriously.

Stephen's dark gaze hardened as he stared at Will.

"Fine," Will said. "Stephen knew Gabi's company was struggling and that her father had just heard he had cancer. He made her a deal that Aurora would invest and save the company, in exchange for a sham marriage." He looked at his mother and his gaze softened. "For Stephen's part, he was worried about you. You have grieved so hard. He thought, rather foolishly, that a wife and perhaps a baby would help with your grief."

Aurora rarely looked shocked but she did now. "Stephen. If that was the case, why didn't you marry Bridget?"

Stephen's voice was as cold as chipped ice. "Because she was a money-grubbing liar who wanted Aurora, Inc., money and a title to show off."

"Bridget was the one who broke Stephen's heart, not Gabi," Will said. "And I was sent to clean up the mess after the wedding. Only Gabi and I…we fell in love."

Stephen made a scoffing noise that had every person in the room looking at him.

Bella spoke softly. "Just because you're hurt doesn't mean everyone else deserves to be."

Will swallowed against a lump in his throat. "I know you're thinking Gabi should trust me, but there are reasons she doesn't that have nothing to do with me. Those are her secrets and she entrusted them to me, which she is probably regretting at this moment. Stephen, I told you in Italy that family is first, and that I will always owe you a debt because of what you did for me years ago. But this…what you did last night did not put family first. You put your hurt feelings and pride first. I'm ashamed of you, Stephen. And it kills me to say that. You're my big brother and I love you."

"I got you out of that flat in London so you could make something of yourself."

Will stood taller. "And I did. And I'm sorry if you don't like who I've become, or if it threatens you in some way. But I'm never going back to being that person. I will always owe you a debt but not on these terms, Stephen. Not when you're so very wrong."

His insides quivered as he faced down his

brother, but it was time. Time he stepped into his own power and agency.

"You have every right to be angry, Will." This from Aurora.

"You all should know that after Stephen spoke to Gabi last night, I made the error of offering to help Baresi out of my own wealth. She turned me down flat. She's not in this for money."

Charlotte got up and went to Will, and hugged him. "I was so awful to you two in Paris."

"We expected it. Falling for each other made everything so complicated and messy."

Christophe finally chipped in. "What are you going to do now?"

"I don't know." He finally sat down and wilted a bit, now that the truth was out and the family knew it all. "I've never...damn. I've never felt like this."

Stephen walked out of the room.

Aurora sighed and looked at Will. "I'll talk to him later. He's hurting more than I realized. It doesn't excuse his behavior. I had no idea, William." She looked over the rest of the children. "I miss your papa every day, but please, do not make any more decisions to protect me or somehow coddle me. I'm fine."

She got up and went to sit beside Will. "I confess I have my doubts. The whole situation is unorthodox. But I am the last person to judge. If you love her, that's good enough for me."

"*Merci*, Maman." He fought the urge to lean in to her shoulder like he would have as a child.

"You really love her?" This from Charlotte.

"Yes. And she loves me, except she doesn't trust herself."

"Then leave this to Bella and me. What this needs is a grand gesture. And if there's anything this family is good at, it's grandeur."

"I'm not sure I want to trust my future happiness to my sisters."

Bella laughed. "Don't worry. We're going to do the dirty work, but you're going to be in it the entire way. You just have to follow our instructions to the letter."

One week later

Gabi stepped into her office and put down her briefcase, ready to start her day. While her heart was bruised and aching, she was feeling ever so much better about Baresi. When she'd returned to the villa, she'd told all to her father. She hadn't wanted to burden him before, but something Will had said once kept coming back to her. About how being involved might be exactly what her father needed. He'd been right. Massimo had been fretting while she'd been trying to protect him. Now they consulted on everything, with her in the office to execute, and she was discovering they made very good partners.

There was a knock on the office door and she went to answer it. She had no meetings this morning, so she wasn't sure who to expect. Opening it to find Charlotte and Bella in front of her was a shock.

"Please hear us out," Charlotte said, stepping just inside the door. "I owe you the biggest apology. Bella and I are here to help."

Curiosity won out, particularly if the antagonistic Charlotte was apologizing.

"I'm not sure there's anything to help," she replied, but she gestured to the two guest chairs in her office. She went to hers behind the desk, needing its protection and illusion of power.

"Stephen was wrong. We all know he spoke to you the night of the party and made you doubt Will. And that Will unwittingly played into the problem by offering to help with Baresi. We're here to assure you that Aurora isn't going to give you one penny." Charlotte grinned. "You're a strong, smart woman and can handle this on your own. What we need help with is handling Will."

Bella jumped in. "He's moping around like someone kicked his dog. You broke his heart, Gabi. He keeps saying he understands why you don't trust him and even Maman has had a go at Stephen for meddling and being a git."

Gabi didn't know what to say. "I don't think it's that simple," she replied.

Bella's dark eyes were sympathetic. "Will says

you have a good reason for not trusting people, but I want you to think back over your relationship. Other than the night of the party, had he ever given you any reason to doubt?"

Gabi knew he hadn't. It was part of what scared her so much.

"I know I was awful to you in Paris, but I didn't know all that about your engagement to Stephen."

"I should never have agreed to it. In the end, I couldn't go through with it. I couldn't marry someone I didn't love, not even to help my family. I thought that was the only way, you know? But now..." She looked around the office. "I have a bit more confidence in my business abilities. My personal life? Not so much."

"Trust is a hard thing to fix," Bella agreed softly. "But if any Baresi involvement is off the table, and Will still wants to be with you...would you be willing to work it out?"

She wanted to so badly she ached with it. In the days since, she'd had a chance to think about it, away from the drama of the Pemberton family. The only person who ever seemed to have an agenda was Stephen, and she was disappointed in him. But even though he'd had an agenda, he'd never lied to her. Not until that night. The arrangement had been clear and she'd agreed to it. His behavior the night of the party had been awful, but Will...she was starting to think her trust hadn't been misplaced. Indeed, she'd rather felt she'd ruined everything since he hadn't even called since she left Chatsworth. After all, she'd leveled him with an accusation and then…run. Again.

Charlotte leaned forward. "Gabi, we have a plan. If you're willing, we're pretty sure we know how you can get Will back…if you want him. You just need your passport, a plane ticket and a killer dress." She handed over an ivory envelope. "You're invited to the Aurora party at the Four Seasons."

CHAPTER FIFTEEN

WILL HAD BEEN a bundle of nerves all day. As head of the fashion division, Paris Fashion Week was a big deal, particularly to Aurora's bottom line. Charlotte had shouldered much of the work on the ground for the first time, and she'd done a fantastic job. The show had been a success and the applause spectacular as Aurora had taken the stage beside a team of designers at the end. As Will watched, happy to be in the background, he realized what a dynamic, strong, amazing woman his mother was.

No wonder his father had fallen for her. She'd taken an idea and made it into an empire. Sure, being married to the Earl of Chatsworth had helped. But he knew that it came down to her vision and strength.

It reminded him of someone else he knew.

Charlotte and Bella had gone to visit Gabi and put their plan in motion, this grand gesture that they seemed to think would fix everything. His palms started to sweat as fear made its way through the elation of the day. What if she didn't come? What if she said no?

He'd missed her with a keenness that robbed him of breath. If she said no now, if it was over for good, he wasn't sure he'd ever be able to breathe again.

After the show, William slid inside the limousine with Aurora, who was glowing, and they departed for the Aurora, Inc., party at the Four Seasons in the massive, ornate ballroom.

"You look beautiful, Maman." She'd chosen an elegant gown in white that draped and shimmered beautifully against her creamy skin. He recognized the Pemberton diamonds at her throat and felt a tightness at his own as he thought of his father. He reached over and took her hand, then kissed the top of it. "I'm so proud of you. Papa would be, too."

"Likewise, darling. I know you doubted I'd put you in the right spot, but look at what we achieved tonight."

"I wish Papa was here to see it."

"Me, too, darling. Me, too. But let's have fun tonight, yes?"

His mother didn't know what he had planned, or she wouldn't have suggested something so lighthearted. His future lay in the balance.

They got out of the limo at the hotel and were immediately faced with camera flashes. A few waves and smiles and they were inside, moving toward the party. There was just one thing missing for Will...or rather one person. Having Gabi here tonight would make it complete.

They were in the foyer before the ballroom, surrounded by icons and the highest fashion in the world, when a simple black dress caught his eye.

And there she was, standing between Charlotte and Bella, wearing Charlotte's black gown—the one Gabi had seen in Milan. It suited her perfectly. The jersey draped over the curve of her hips and fell to the floor in soft folds, and the halter neckline highlighted the column of her throat and her strong, beautiful shoulders. Her hair was up and...he swallowed thickly. Bella had loaned her jewelry. He recognized the diamond-and-pearl teardrop earrings that their father had given her on her eighteenth birthday.

She'd come.

Charlotte gave Gabi a gentle nudge, and she looked startled for a moment, but then began walking across the foyer toward him, her dark eyes wide and unsure, her lip...oh, she was biting her lip. Did she not realize he would welcome her with open arms?

He glanced to his left... Aurora had melted away into the background. Out of his way.

And then Gabi was there, before him, so incredibly beautiful he wasn't sure he knew how to breathe.

"You're here," he said, feeling at once stupid and awestruck. "You never said for sure if you were coming."

She laughed. "I wasn't sure. But then I decided that I had to stop running away. Though I might have had some help with that." She looked over her shoulder at his sisters, who grinned ridiculously and gave them a thumbs-up. She laughed, and he thought he'd never heard such a gorgeous sound in his life.

"My sisters can be persuasive."

She met his gaze. "I didn't want to listen. I was afraid to listen, Will. And the more I thought about it, the more I realized I'd panicked because of my insecurities, and not because of you."

"I would never... Oh, Gabi. I would never seduce you for business. It's just not in me. Every feeling, every kiss, every touch...it was all you. None of it was part of my plan. I only offered what I did to help. Not because of what Stephen said. He lied to you. He said so in front of the entire family."

"In front of everyone?"

"When you left, I called a family meeting."

Her gaze widened. "Your sisters never told me that."

"I should have done it earlier. I should have spoken up the night before when everyone was being so awful. I didn't stand up for you, Gabi, so I can hardly blame you for doubting me."

She touched his hand and her fingers shook against his. "I was so afraid. That evening was so hard. And then Stephen… It hit on a weakness and I was already vulnerable. I should have been stronger for you, like you were for me. I'm so sorry, Will. Sorry I ran instead of staying for us to work it out like I said I would."

"If Stephen hadn't—"

"No," she interrupted. "That's my fault, not your brother's. The truth is, I'm stronger than I realized and a good deal of that is due to you. I hope you…" She cleared her throat. "I hope you forgive me."

"Of course I forgive you. I love you."

"Oh, Will, I love you, too. I'm so sorry I was such a fool."

Will no longer cared about scandals or paparazzi or public displays of affection. Right now, the only thing that mattered was the woman in front of him, and he cupped his hands around her face and kissed her, the ache in his chest replaced by a sweetness he'd never known.

She was here. She still loved him. Charlotte and Bella had done their part, and now it was his turn. He looked over his shoulder at his mother, standing ten feet behind him and smiling. Another look around showed Christophe and Lizzy next to Bella and Charlotte. The only one missing was Stephen, and for that Will found he was a bit sad.

But the time was right. He felt it in his heart. "Gabi?"

"What is it?"

He took her hand in his. "I love you, you know that, right?"

She nodded, her eyes warm and affectionate.

"And we've already shown we can make it through high-pressure situations."

She laughed then. "Oh, one or two. Never mind the pictures that will probably be online in about five seconds because you kissed me in a public ballroom."

He reached inside his pocket and took out a box. It was white satin with black trim around it, the classic Aurora packaging. It had taken him three hours to decide on the one he wanted, and his heart beat frantically in his chest at what he was about to do. "Will you do me the honor of marrying me? Because I don't think I can do this alone anymore."

He opened the box and inside was nestled a stunning oval engagement ring with channel-set diamonds on either side.

For three whole, torturous seconds, Gabi stood with her hand over her mouth in stunned surprise.

And then her arms were around his neck as she hugged him close. "Oh," she cried softly. "Oh, William. I didn't expect this."

"Is that a yes?" His arms tightened around her.

"Yes." She let him go and moved back enough

that she could look up at him. Her eyes were wet with tears but her lips were smiling. "Yes. But please, can we not get married in the Chatsworth chapel?"

He laughed. "Deal." And then he took the ring out of the box and slid it over her finger as a cheer went up from the crowd.

"This is so not going to be discreet," she lamented.

"This time, I don't give a damn." He kissed her hand. "I love you and I don't care who knows it."

They spent a few minutes accepting congratulations from the family, and others who seemed more curious than anything. Finally Gabi pulled on his sleeve. "I should call Mama and Papa and tell them the news," she said. "They both thought I was crazy for leaving you, anyway."

"Of course."

She was just about to head to a quieter spot when he tugged on her fingers. "Gabi? We won't set a date until we're sure your father can walk you down the aisle. In Italy. The wedding will be in your home." Then he thought of the villa, and how they'd truly fallen in love in Italy, and he added, "In our home."

And when she walked away to share the good news, he knew all the missing pieces suddenly fit together.

* * * * *